T0198655

Catharine's Diary

Catharine's Diary

The 1919 life of a 10-year old near Woodstock NY

Catharine Snyder Mortensen
and
Jim Mortensen

iUniverse, Inc.
New York Bloomington

Catharine's Diary

The 1919 life of a 10-year old near Woodstock NY

iUniverse books may be ordered through booksellers or by contacting:

iUniverse
1663 Liberty Drive
Bloomington, IN 47403
www.iuniverse.com
1-800-Authors (1-800-288-4677)

ISBN: 978-1-4401-6287-9 (pbk)
ISBN: 978-1-4401-6289-3 (ebk)

Printed in the United States of America

iUniverse rev. date: 9/16/2009

Dedication

To my grandchildren, Catharine's great grandchildren, Catharine Lewis and Soren Mortensen: Remember in order to know where you are going; you have to learn where you've been.

Introduction and a Promise Kept

After my mother, Catharine Mortensen, nee Snyder, died on March 31, 2008, I discovered her diaries among her things. For a time, she was a compulsive diarist, keeping daily logs continually from January, 1936 through May, 1956 when she abruptly stopped. So meticulous was she about making entries that she even had my father do them while she was in the hospital giving birth to both of her sons—her second, my brother Harold, was born by C-section which, in 1940, necessitated an especially long hospital stay. Prior to that series, however, she kept only one diary, her first, for the year 1919.

It was the 1919 diary that especially interested me —although I eventually expect to read through them all—for two reasons. First, because 1919 was the year she turned 10; the age my grandchildren (her great grand children) were at the time of her death. The second, because it was during this year that her father, Leonard, suffered some sort of mental breakdown that caused the family to commit him to an asylum, a story that was never fully explained. So it was that, after reading through the diary of a 10-year old growing up in Pine Grove, under Overlook Mountain, in New York's Catskill Mountains, I decided to try, as best I could, to transcribe this diary and tell her story for succeeding generations of her family.

In addition I made her a promise. At one point during her early nineties she said to me "When I'm gone, you will forget about me." I promised her that was not going to happen. What follows is part of keeping that promise.

Cover photograph of Catharine and Carlo is undated but probably taken in 1918.

The Family History

To best understand the family it is necessary to look at its history, and the Snyders have had a long one in North America. The original of Catharine's line of Schneider or Snyder—it was apparently changed either just before or when the family immigrated—was Martin who was transported via England to North America in 1725. He and his fellow refugees were originally from the principality of Rhineland-Palatine: one of the hundred or so small principalities that formed after the 30-Years War had torn the Germanic peoples of Northern Europe asunder. It wouldn't be part of Germany again until the country was reunited by Bismarck in 1871.

Martin was a part of a group of Protestants that, having been displaced by the series of ongoing wars between, primarily, Protestant England and Catholic France, had become wards of England's Queen Anne. (There were Catholics mixed in as well but if the passenger listings in regard to religion are correct less than 25 percent practiced this religion.) Not wanting to allow this people's particular brands of Lutheranism or Calvinism to contaminate that of the Church of England plus dealing with famine brought on by the Little Ice Age, Anne struck a deal with Robert Livingstone to populate his holdings in the Hudson Valley with this particular group of Palatines. (Others had already been relocated to Ireland and the Carolinas.) The intention of this forced relocation was that the Palatines would, besides enriching Livingstone's holdings and forming a buffer between the English colony and the French/Indians, manufacture stores of pitch and tar for the British Navy. Once here, however, the Palatines found the North American pines left a lot to be desired when it came to producing naval stores and that they would rather settle and farm for themselves than weave hemp rope, cut pine trees and boil sap for the British. Much to the dismay of Patroon Livingstone and defying his authority, they spread out along the Hudson, up the Mohawk into the area around Canajoharie and southward into New Jersey and Pennsylvania.

Here is a bit of a historic notation/correction: The Palatines were of Germanic descent who spoke *Deutsch* or High German. They were not the nationality of people who came from The Netherlands or Holland which are referred to as Dutch and whose language is, more correctly, *Nederland* or Middle German. The languages spoken by the Palatines and the Hollanders might have, to the untrained, nonGermanic ear, sounded alike but the peoples that spoke them came from two distinctly different areas of Europe. While New York was originally a colony of Holland it was not widely settled by the Dutch per se, rather the colony was ruled from Amsterdam and settled by people from a variety of countries. Since most of the early colonists were merchant/traders of many nationalities that either set up shop in New Amsterdam (New York City) or Fort Orange (Albany) while fairly much ignoring the rest, there were few true Hollanders in the colony. When the British forced the surrender of New Amsterdam in 1674, aside from western Long Island, most of the land in the colony was empty of people other than a few farmers living along the river between the two cities, or Native Americans. An example would be

Kingston which was a small trading fort known as Esopus clinging to the edge of the Hudson. It wasn't until the elder Robert Livingstone was awarded a grant to buy a large section of land in the midHudson Valley from the Native Americans that the Germans who spoke *Deutsch* were brought in. Somehow, probably because of their language, these people were later referred to as Dutch, most likely from an English bastardization of the word *Deutsch* and it was assumed those who spoke it were from Holland. The name stuck—i.e. the Pennsylvanian Dutch are likewise of German, many of Palatine, descent—even reached the point where later generations thought of themselves as Dutch. (My mother often insisted her parents were Dutch and spoke Dutch among themselves a language that she managed to learn well enough by age six to discover there was no such thing as Santa Claus. It wasn't until the genealogy of her family tree was shown to her that was she convinced otherwise. I suspect what she thought was Dutch was actually the Germanic sounding language unique to the area and what Alf Evers, in his book on Woodstock, refers to as New York State Dutch.) At any rate, unless someone can trace their New York family tree back to the 1660's or to a more recent emigrate from Holland, chances are fairly good that a Germanic name from pre-Revolutionary New York means their ancestors were Palatines, not Dutch. (Most of those original New Amsterdam families, by the way, have kept a fairly comprehensive genealogical track of their family trees.)

Martin Snyder, like the majority of those who arrived in the 1720's, stayed closer to his original landing site—probably West Camp, NY. He eventually established his farm on the west side of the Hudson just outside of Saugerties near where, some two and a half centuries later, a huge group of counter-cultural hippies created a happening called "Woodstock". (This is another misnomer as the actually village of Woodstock is over 10 miles from the site.) It was here, with his second wife, Anna, (the first having died in childbirth back in Europe) that these first American Snyders brought forth fourteen children who, amazingly, all lived to adulthood. This, in and of itself, was a marvel for the day and gave the family a running start in populating the area, but even more amazing, the last two were twins boys born in 1750 when Anna was 47. The Snyder females would prove to have long fertility cycles.

By the time the Revolutionary War came to the Hudson Valley, Martin's farm was established and his family was well on its way. Excepting the twins and a couple of sons, the Snyder children were married and had established homesteads of their own by the outbreak of the war. As will happen in any "civil" war, family's loyalties differ and sons join opposite sides. One son, Jeremiah, like most of the rest of the family, threw in with the rebels and rose to a captaincy in the Whig or American army probably as an "irregular" watching for British/Indian attacks coming from over the Catskills from Canada. An older brother, by seven years, Zachariah was the only family member to stay loyal to the British and became a Tory captain. Whether they ever fought each other is not recorded but in 1780, Jeremiah and his 18-year old son, Elias, were captured by Indians loyal to the British, marched from the Catskills to Fort Niagara and imprisoned. They later escaped while on parole in the St. Lawrence Valley and made their way, via Vermont and Massachusetts, back to the Hudson Valley. As far as Zachariah is concerned his war record was not known, but after the peace was signed and because he was on the losing side, he was exiled to Nova Scotia. Later he would return to the country of his birth, settling in New Jersey where he married and sired eleven children. While all stayed close to home, there was one exception. His third oldest daughter, Margaret, went back into the Hudson Valley where she met and married Frederick Cunyes. Four generations later, Jeremiah's great, great, grandson and the great grandson of Elias, was Leonard Snyder who would become Catharine's father. In 1883 Leonard married Irene Cunyes who was, without either of them knowing it, the great, great granddaughter of Zachariah and Leonard's fourth cousin. Thus Catharine and her siblings would be able to claim that their great, great, great grandfathers both fought in the Revolutionary War but on opposite sides and, that they were brothers to boot.

The kind of inbreeding is not that unusual for the Palatine families as they tended to be very self-contained communities that tended to marry within their own group—the family name of Fiero appears and reappears in the Snyder family tree as well. By way of example, of five of Leonard and Irene's children who married, only one, Catharine, married someone who had not been born and brought up in the northeastern part of Ulster County, NY. By way of contrast, of their 14 grandchildren who married, at least half married outside the Palatine culture. Like the rest of America, the Palatines were on the move.

The Immediate Family

The Parents

Leonard Snyder or **Pa** or **Pop** was born on May 12, 1859 and died on August 9, 1920—the year after this diary was written. He was the sixth child, fourth son, of the ten children (four girls) born to Elias Snyder and Eliza Lasher Snyder. (It is easy to be confused on the names Jeremiah and Elias as they, as well as Martin, appear all over the family tree—actually Leonard's grandfather was Jeremiah Elias Snyder.) These ten children survived childhood but not all married. I don't know much about the family's home but I do know they had a farm in Pine Grove just up from where Catharine was born. Most likely their life was typical of the residents of the area in that they worked in the local forest or bluestone quarries to supplement whatever cash their produce brought in. I do know that Leonard, besides his own farm, worked for most of his adult life at the bluestone quarries and drove wagonloads of the cut stone down the mountain on the Plattekill Clove Road. This is was not a job for the careless or cowards since this particularly steep slope required chaining the wagon's wheels to keep the heavy loads under control and necessitated constant pouring of water on the wooden brakes so they didn't ignite from the friction. By 1919 it appeared, at age 60, that he no longer worked at this job but kept to his farm and helped neighbors on theirs.

Irene Cunyes Snyder, **Mother**, was the born on January 10, 1863 and died on January 1, 1947. She was the older of two daughters of Sanford Cunyes and Sarah Herrick Cunyes. I know very little about where she grew up or what her family did except that her family home was in Pine Grove and named "Shagbark" for the number of hickory trees around it. The home was near the home where she and Leonard were living in 1919. I suspect that neither she nor Leonard ever moved more than 5 miles from their birthplaces prior to starting their family. Inasmuch as she and Leonard were both members of the Pine Grove community it probably had not been hard for her to meet him. They were married the last day of October, 1883. Like all women of her era, she was able to care for a home by cooking, canning, gardening and sewing. She was especially good at crocheting, a skill she would teach her youngest daughter before she turned ten.

The Siblings:

Maude Esther was the born on December 17, 1884. On May 16, 1912 she married Jessie Mower and left home. By 1919 she had already given birth to 5 of her 10 children, 2 of whom had died as infants. Because she was so much older than Catharine and out of the house by the time Catharine turned three, there wasn't much contact between them. For whatever reason, Maude had little contact with the rest of the family except when they visited her, something that seemed to continue into later life. In fact, given the ages of Maude and Jessie's children, Catharine would be closer to them than their parents. Maude would die in 1957.

Arthur (Art) Elias was born on May 22, 1887. I remember him as being tall and lanky. Aside from the usual farm chores as a boy, he worked with his father at the quarries and was one of those who poured water on the brakes. By 1919 he had married **Eva Dora** Russell from over the hill near Hurley and was working in Newburgh. They never had children but owned one of the first pug dogs that I had ever seen. In their later years they came back to the Russell family farm located on NYS Route 375 between West Hurley and Woodstock and lived with Eva Dora's maiden sister, Lydia. (For years, until I saw family genealogy, I though Art's wife's name was a single word, Evadora like Catharine spelled it, since that is the way the family always referred to her. It was also pronounced ev-aah dora not ee-vah dora.) I remember the Route 375 house as being located in the middle of an elongated 90-degree, "S" curve in such a way that people were always driving cars into the white picket fence that bordered the road—a bar at the top of the hill probably contributing to some of these accidents. Art had a kind of cottage industry that centered on collecting money from motorists for repairs to this fence. It seemed that it was always in need of repair from the latest accident or had been just repaired from the last one. Aside from that, he kept a cow, a few chickens, and some pigs and "farmed" after a fashion, mostly in an attempt to keep the forest from taking over his fields. Sometime after he died on January 10, 1972 the state bought the house, demolished it and straightened the road. The only reminder is a pond where the barn once stood, fed by the barn's spring that was used to cool the milk.

Luther (Lute) Cunyes was born on April 17, 1889. I remember him as being the opposite in build of his older brother. In 1911 he married **Cora** Belle Elting who was also born and raised near Woodstock. They had one son, Luther Erwin, called **Erwin**, born in 1917. Luther's life was a real Horatio Alger story. As a 17-year old in 1906 and with just an eighth grade education, he began working for the New York Central Railroad as a busboy selling sandwiches to passengers in the station at Kingston. Two years later he was transferred to an office job in Albany. By 1913 he had, through hard work and an ability to organize, risen to chief clerk of the NYCRR's New York division of dining service and was relocated to Buffalo. In 1936 he, Cora and Erwin moved to Chicago when he was promoted to assistant superintendent of dining services for all of the NYCRR from Buffalo to St. Louis. He would retire from the NYCRR in 1954 as Chief of Dining Car Service. Whenever my family would travel from our home in New York State to visit my father's family in Minnesota we would stop on the way out at Lute's in Chicago. As soon as we arrived and after we had spent two days sitting in the car, the first thing Lute would do was to load us into his car and give us a tour of the city. On the other hand, when my brother and I, as preteens, traveled to Minnesota by train, he made sure a porter met us in Albany and looked after us all the way to Chicago where Uncle Lute met us at the station and saw that we made the right connections. The same occurred on the return trip. Lute passed away on January 6, 1970.

Ernest (Ernie) Leonard was born on July 16, 1891. By all accounts Ernie was a normal baby but sometime during his early years, probably as the result of some childhood disease, his mental development stopped. In today's parlance, Ernie was "special". From all my contact with him and by talking to those that knew him, it seems he probably reached a preteen in his mental development but was in every way very socially adept and trainable—he was a demon at the game of dominoes for one thing and loved to beat his nieces and nephews. By 1919 he was away from home working one of his many menial farm jobs, something he did until his death on January 26, 1968. I remember being with my parents when they picked him up at one of his jobs as a gardener's assistant in a complex of greenhouses near Kingston. He gave us a tour of the facility and showed us what he did. From everything we've ever heard he was an excellent worker who took pride in what he could do.

Elizabeth (Liz or Lizzie) Irene was born on July 14, 1893 and was the baby girl of the family until Catharine came along. This meant the chore of taking care of a baby sister who was 16 years her junior, fell to her. This job, the taking care of members of the family, would never end. In later years—sometime before 1936 as per Catharine's later diaries—she came to be called Betty and it is as Aunt Betty or Aunt B that she is best remembered by two successive generations of nieces, nephews and their offspring. As soon as she finished grade school, maybe even before, she began work as a house maid, chamber maid, waitress or whatever employment was available to a young woman at that time. She worked first locally in hotels in the area but by 1919, having turned 26; she moved out to seek employment away from home. Later in life she settled in Kingston where she worked in the shirt factory until retirement. Not being able to slow down, however, she continued in odd jobs of many sorts—I remember for a couple of years in the mid '50's she ran the concession stand at a drive-in. It was at her home, first on Smith Ave and later on Elmendorf, that she offered tough love, great fried chicken and popcorn (there was always a big tub of it on the stove) to nieces and nephews. She, for whatever reason, never married and it became her lot in life to be the one that took care of her mother until Irene's death. This chore did not slow her down as she traveled widely from the Thousand Islands to Florida to California and Vegas, sometime working in hotels, but mostly as a tourist who knew how to enjoy herself. Aunt Betty may well have been a women's libber back when the movement didn't have a name. She died in 1985, just 12 days short of her 92nd birthday.

Raymond (Ray) Tracy was the last of Leonard and Irene's sons, born on November 19, 1898. As the last boy, with his older brothers off on their own by 1919 and his father beginning to show signs of mental deterioration, it was the 21-year old Ray's job to keep their farm running. Not only was his labor needed at home but what room and board he paid to his parents certainly helped subsidize the family. He worked a number of different farm jobs in the area where, apparently, there was a growing number of dairy operations coming into being. Determined not to go into the bluestone mines—although he helped as a preteen with watering the brakes on the wagons—he would eventually work in a bluestone dock as a stonecutter of cemetery memorials. I can remember his "trademark"; two fingers that were shortened when a crane lowering an especially large stone dropped it on to his hand. The story was that he took off his glove after the accident and the end of his fingers rolled out. In 1921 he would marry one of his sister Elizabeth's best friends, **Orpha Bishop**—she who two years earlier had given Catharine her first diary. Their first child, a daughter who was named Elizabeth, died within two days of her birth but they would go on to have four more, three sons and a daughter. Ray, because he was closest to Catharine in age was probably the closest to her in the family, and it was he and Orpha who would stand up with her when she married. Like his mother and all of older brothers, Ray passed away in January on the 9th of that month in1973.

The Diarist

If you have been keeping track you will have noticed that Leonard and Irene's progeny came along at fairly uniform intervals of about two years, slowing down just slightly with the 5 years between Elizabeth and Raymond. (My mother told me once that there may well have been a miscarriage in there which, if true, would explain the gap.) You can imagine then the surprise that occurred when, nearly 11 years after Ray's birth and at the age of 45, Irene found she was pregnant. In fact, Catharine was to be forever known in the family as "the Little Surprise". (Remember I said earlier that Snyder women—which Irene was—had long fertility periods. Something I am including here as a warning to later generations.)

Catharine May—she could have been named for any number of preceding Catharines, Catherines, Katherines, Katrinas or Kates that appear in the family line—came into the world on February 25, 1909. (For most of her life she had problems with other people misspelling her name but on her baptism certificate it is Catharine with an "a".) Her story was that she was born on the kitchen table, something I still take with a grain of salt, but, like all births in those days, she was born in the Snyder home in Pine Grove probably in her mother's bed. The world she came into was a bit different than that of her siblings because she was so much younger than those who preceded her. Her sister Elizabeth was 16 and certainly able to help her mother with the baby. Additionally, there were other, older brothers who were in and out of the house, some with girl friends interested in becoming part of the family. All were willing to spoil this child. She also had an 11-year older brother to keep an eye on her. In spite of the family's economic condition, she was better off than most children born in 1909.

I have no doubt that she was spoiled. For one thing she was the first and only child in the family to take piano lessons and, as a result, trotted out at family affairs to play for those assembled. Then there was her hair. We have only one set of colored pictures of her made before she reached the Clairol stage of her life, a 15 minute, 8mm movie shot in 1941. In it one can see that not only was her hair a brilliant red but her complexion matched it. Also, I remember her saying she was called "Carrot Top" in grade school which is pretty indicative of her hair color then. At any rate, whether the red hair was a sign of a temper or whether she was told she should have a temper because she had red hair, she knew what she wanted and made sure she got it. I am sure this started early and, if you read her diary carefully, you can see that she wasn't denied much.

So, in 1919, we have a ten-year old who has been brought up pretty much by parents much closer in age to grandparents with few children of her age to play with. She is used to expecting and getting gifts when she wants them. Not that she was not willing to work hard, she may well have been one of the hardest workers on menial jobs like berry picking and gardening that anyone has ever known, but she also did things her own way. On top of that she is extremely intelligent and, in some areas at least, insightful. Finally, a trait that will stay with her throughout her life, she is deeply religious.

The Rest of the Cast

It was not until Catharine's generation and, to a larger extent the one that followed, that the Snyder's moved away from Pine Grove and out of Ulster County. As I said above, Leonard and Irene lived less than five miles from where they were born and this was true of most of their siblings. Since this meant that many were a part of Catharine's life and appear in her diary, I will try to identify them as best as memory, genealogy and cemetery records allow. I have taken the liberty of highlighting those names that appear in the diary. Keep in mind, however, some are pure guesses since there were pet family names as well as duplicate ones—Catharines, Marys and Kates abound and to avoid confusion some go by middle names. Some, who make brief appearances or aren't identifiable, will be noted in the transcribed diary. Others who are more important, I've listed here in boldface.

The Snyder's:

Aunt Mary: Mary Catharine the oldest of Leonard's siblings and had actually married a Snyder, presumably from another branch of the family. She had a son, Elbert which Catharine seems to have spelled **Albert** and a daughter May **Viola**. Elbert was married to Eliza or **Lila** and had a son, **Lester**.

Uncle Will: William L Snyder Leonard's oldest brother who was married **Aunt Ida** Wolven. They had two daughters, Hattie and **Grace**.

Uncle Raym: Raymond Snyder, an older, bachelor brother who lived nearby.

Uncle Chester or Ches: was Lemuel Chester Snyder a bachelor brother of Leonard. He lived just up the hill from Leonard with Raym. These two brothers were referred to as the "Bachelors" know for their beards which, as Catharine remembered, always were tobacco stained.

Aunt Martha: Leonard's closest sister— 2 years older—and married to William Burton who—this is why this is confusing—may also have been called **Uncle Will.**

Uncle Charlie or Char: Charles Raymond Snyder, Leonard's younger brother, by 3 years, and married to **Aunt Jane or Janey**. They had a daughter, **Mabel** and granddaughter, **Marion.**

Uncle Frank or Franklin: another of Leonard's younger brothers. He was also, probably, the most ambitious, having moved all the way to Saugerties where he and **Aunt Lilie** started the Saugerties branch of the family. Two of his older daughters, **Bernice** and **Lauretta,** and two oldest sons **Herman** and **Orville** are mentioned in the diary.

Uncle Meyer: Leonard's youngest brother, David Myer Snyder who was married to Aunt Katherine—also **Aunt Kate**. They had a daughter **Anna** who would have been 6 in 1919.

(The list of Leonard's siblings is in chronological order in terms of their birth order. Two of Leonard's sisters, Julia and Jane, had died in 1917 and 1911, respectively, so did not reckon into this period.)

Peter Snyder: Leonard's first cousin was the son of Leonard's Uncle William and was about the same age as Leonard. Peter was probably Leonard's closest friend and was his best man when Leonard and Irene were married.

The Cunyes'

Aunt Esther: Irene's younger sister, by four years, and only sibling. She had a son, **Harry** Pierce, who would have been about 28 in 1919. There is a question as to whether she and the boy's father ever married but either way, he had deserted her. In 1919 she was living in Kingston. I know that, at some point in her life, she became extremely deaf and relied on an ear trumpet to hear.

Addie or Adline: Margaret Adeline Herrick Snyder daughter of Mary Cunyes Herrick who was Irene's aunt, a sister of Sanford. (Whether it was because of pronunciation or just her way of spelling, Catharine decided Adeline's name should be Adline.) She had married a Snyder who was a fourth cousin of Leonard's and had died prior to 1919. Her granddaughter, **Dorthea** or **Dot Merkel**, was a year older than Catharine and probably one of her best friends growing up. Dot's mother's name was **Mabel** and she had another son, **Crawford**, who appears in the diary.

Helen K: Helen Herrick Kiersted also known as Helly and a first cousin of Irene.

Uncle Dewitt: Dewitt Croswell who was married to Catherine Adelia Cunyes and was probably also called **Aunt Kate**. Their grandchildren, **Irving** and **Iva** who would have been about 6 and 5, respectively, were children of their oldest son Roy.

Aunt Sarah and **Aunt Joan** were wives of Sanford's brothers so were Irene's aunts by marriage.

(Note at some point, later in their history, some members of the family name changed their surname to Conyers.)

The Others:

Mr. and Mrs. Richter—another name that Catharine spelled various ways—were just close friends and members of the Christ Lutheran Church who, apparently, lived in the area on a seasonal basis.

Floyd and Ella Burton: relatives of William Burton.

Mr. Sheltise, probably correctly spelled Shultis, is a fairly common name in the area and was Catharine's great grandmother's maiden name. He may well be related. Shultis Corners is the name of an area between Pine Grove and Woodstock.

Bratt were neighbors who eventually moved to New Jersey.

Stoll was a neighbor whose family name was known well enough that the road which went by Leonard and Irene's house still bears it.

Pine Grove

If you were to look for Pine Grove on a road map of Ulster County New York, you will not find it listed although it does appear on the topographic map of the county. There are, according to a listings of topographic maps actually 5 Pine Groves in New York State and if you Google Pine Grove, NY, you will get the one located in the western Adirondacks. The Pine Grove of the Snyder's was not a place but a location or a community, that was a loose collection of related families, primarily of Palatine stock, where the name meant something to them but it was neither a village nor town. If you were to ask the people in 1919 where they lived they would probably have said either Ulster County or, more than likely, Woodstock. If you asked them for their mailing address and you would have gotten a rural Saugerties address. In actuality they were about half way between the two locations—about seven miles in either direction along, what is now New York Route 212. The only sign locally that now indicates Pine Grove's existence is a street, Pine Grove Avenue, on whose corner with Band Camp Road and old State Route 212, stands the Pine Grove School house.

The Pine Grove School was not only the area's educational institution; it was the community's center. A small, two-room building, constructed of clapboard and local stone, it was where a generation of Snyder's and their kith and kin got a smattering of education up through grade 8 and then were sent out into the world of work. This was assuming, of course, that the child was allowed to graduate before being removed from school because the child's labor was needed at home, their income was needed by the family, or, they had threatened the teacher and been expelled. The school stands one and seven tenths miles east of Leonard and Irene's house on a single lane dirt road. It is a long, winding walk for a 5 to 13-year old child; down Stoll Road, then a short distance on Pine Lane and, finally, down Band Camp Road. The daily walk was neither uphill nor down, but a little of both and when it was raining or snowing or temperatures were below zero, certainly a grueling test for one so young. To have made this trip every day for eight years is an indication of how important an education was to Catharine and her siblings.

Aside from the school and the homes scattered on the four main roads: Pine Grove Ave., Pine Lane, Stoll Rd. and Band Camp Rd., there were no other community structures. The Snyder's worshiped seven miles to the south in Woodstock at the Christ Lutheran Church, a trip that probably required an hour or so by horse and wagon or sleigh. Woodstock was a minor town at this point in time, primarily a collection of homes, an inn, and store that supplied those who lived further into the mountains. The Snyder's, if they had to go to "town" or "the village" went east to Saugerties, a mill town on the west bank of the Hudson. Here was the post office and the New York Central Railroad station where they could travel north to Albany and beyond or south to Kingston, Newburgh and New York City. If one needed to go to the "city", they went to Kingston. My mother told me once about a store that stood along Route 212 but it isn't mentioned in her diary so I'll assume it wasn't there in 1919.

The only other thing the community had in common was the Chestnut Hill Cemetery which had been started by Catharine's great grandfather, William Cunyes. Located south of town and east of Woodstock, you could get there fastest by taking Pine Lane It held generations of Palatine descendants. This was the final resting place for many residents of Pine Grove including Irene and Leonard.

I do have a photograph of Pine Grove, a sepia photo, probably from the late 1930's and, it appears to have been taken from along

Stoll Road looking toward the Snyder homestead. The photo has been trimmed from a postcard sent by someone to my mother. This was one of the "things" people did back in that era: one took a photo and had it made into a post card—it saved paper and postage. Unfortunately, the address part and most of the message are missing so I don't know who it is from and what is left of the message doesn't make enough sense to figure it out. Apparently someone, probably my mother, trimmed the card down so they could save just the photo but it gives one an idea of what the area was like.

It shows a one-lane dirt road wandering between fields fenced in by barbed wire, and the remains of a stone wall hidden by roadside weeds. That wall represented the work of generations of Snyder's, Shultis's, Lasher's, Cunyes' or Herrick's or their kin who pried out the rock, loaded it into sledges drawn by oxen or horses and hauled it to the edges of their fields where they laid up the walls. Behind the walls are fields which by this time have grown up to weeds and second growth timber, since it was the Depression and the land was no longer being farmed. There is a stump near the road, probably all that is left of the Chestnuts trees that used to line it.

The road winds off through low hills and past a few white houses. I'm not sure because I wouldn't see this area for another twenty years but it would seem that, in the distance, slightly off to the left before the road winds up the hill is the Leonard Snyder farmstead. There are a couple of buildings sitting close to the road that would have been where their barn was located. Here they stabled the horse and, later, Elizabeth garaged her first car. The house is barely visible through the trees, built against the side of the hill in such a way that the lower floor was cool enough to store hams and vegetables at a time before refrigeration. What I can't see, because the camera, judging by the late afternoon shadows, is pointed more north and east, is Overlook Mountain. This Catskill peak stood a mile or so behind the house and sheltered Pine Grove from the late afternoon sun.

In 1919 the area would have been cleaner; better taken care of and farmed. I remember going up there in the 1950's and my mother pointing out where their pasture had been. It was a forest where no tree had a diameter less than 4 inches and no self-respecting cow could have found enough grass to survive. The house stood uphill from the barn and small stream cut the front yard in half, separating the house from the barn and other outbuildings. It was in that stream where they built the "spring house" to keep things like butter and milk chilled. Next to the house was a tall catalpa tree where katydids sang in the fall evenings, their "Katie Did" calls accusing young Catharine of things she did not do. By 2009 this area was completely grown up, the house nearly invisible from the road and all the fields and pastures given over to maturing second growth pine and hardwoods. Pine Grove was now, in fact, a grove of pines.

It was a good place for kids to grow up. The air was clean and the water fairly pure so disease was kept at bay. The area had been cleared to the point where most major wildlife was gone. Bears were driven back into the Catskills and, by 1919 most of the deer were confined to pockets in the Adirondacks or Catskills where they were getting ready to mount their comeback later in the century. The only wildlife threat was the timber rattler and Catharine grew up scared to death of snakes in any size, shape or color. This was something, along with the fear of water, that she took with her to the grave—the result, I am sure, of constant warnings to a child from overprotective adults with just one baby to worry about.

Back from the road were meadows where, in the late spring, wild strawberries grew if you knew where to find them. These berries, most the size of a current, where hell to hull but the Snyder women picked, hulled and turned them into shortcake or preserves. The swamp and land that had been lumbered off and was too steep or rocky for pasture, tilling or hay, held late summer bounties of high-bush blueberries or huckleberries on shrubs higher than a 10-year old's head, low-bush blueberries, crackers (this was their name for bunchberries, *Cornus canadensis*, a low-growing species of dogwood), nannyberries (*Viburnum lentago* L.), wild grapes and wintergreen berries. Additionally, if you didn't mind the thorns, there were tangles of black and red raspberries as well as blackberries. Along the road and in the yards of some of the houses stood tall hickory and American chestnut trees where, with permission, you could pick up nuts, especially if you had a big brother to thrash (shake) the tree for you. These fruits and nuts were savored fresh and many a winter night was spent with the family sitting around the kitchen table cracking and picking out nutmeats. (They had a special nutcracker, unique to this area and meant especially for hickory nuts, which cracked the nut without smashing the nutmeat. Catharine would inherit one and it would be passed down in the family.) In the spring, the whole family would head to the jointly operated sugar house and boil sap for maple syrup and sugar. Adults, often to the delight the children, tossed the hot, thick syrup on top of the snow to make especially delicious maple candy called dobache.

This was a time before refrigeration and, as far as I can see from the diary, the Snyder's didn't have the luxury of an ice box. (They would use snow for making ice cream and Mom told me once that snow laid in so deep in a spot below Overlook Mountain that they were able to gather it to make ice cream on the Fourth of July.) This meant everything harvested had to be either used fresh or preserved, usually by canning, but it could be smoked or dried. (Catharine doesn't mention a smoke house, but I suspect they or some member of the family had one.) Apparently things had progressed far enough in Pine Grove that there was a traveling grocer who came up from Kingston once a month to deliver those things that could not be grown or were not made on the farm—flour, sugar, etc. The family raised their own pigs, chickens and had a least one cow. Surplus was either sold or traded for what they needed. In the back of the diary Catharine later made a list of berries she picked in the summer of 1922 and sold: 69 quarts of blue, huckle and black berries for a total of $15.25. This was probably a small fortune for a thirteen-year old in 1922 and I expect the money went to her mother.

The family's wants and needs in 1919 were few. They had no electricity or telephone—although, apparently the latter had reached Pine Grove. Long range communication was done by letter and, by all appearances, the service seemed faster then than now. If one needed emergency contact, they sent a telegraph. Local travel was horse and buggy/sleigh or "shanks mare". Although the automobile was coming into use and a few in Pine Grove owned one, excepting for Luther in Buffalo, no Snyder had a car until Betty bought one sometime after 1920. If someone needed to travel long distances they went to Saugerties for the train or to take the bus.

So this was the time and place when 10-year old Catharine began writing in her first diary. The story that follows is hers to tell.

Notes on the Transcription

The diary is a small one, 2.5 by 5 inches, with two day's worth of entries on each page, eight lines per entry. While some entries are short, a few long ones sprawled into the margins and wound up the edge of the page. She wrote in cursive using pencil for most entries with, occasionally, a fountain pen. Sometimes things were erased and redone and ink entries were crossed out. A few of the pencil entries are very faint and smudged. All of this made some of the things which, combined with her penchant for changing spellings, difficult to read even with a magnifying glass.

As far as her grammar and punctuation, I have pretty much gone with what is on the page. I suspect the grammar is that of her time and place. While both her parents were literate—they both had some elementary school education and, as noted in the diary, exchanged letters—they probably weren't too concerned with the correct use of the King's English. I am sure Catharine was just copying what she heard, quite possibly even from her teachers. I do know in later years one of her pet peeves was a minister who insisted on saying "Christ died for you and I." When she heard it, it set her teeth on edge but the diary is full of this kind of usage.

The spellings are also left pretty much as she wrote them. Note there are few, primarily people's names, that differ and I suggest if you get confused, you look back at the listing of people above. If, on the other hand, I could not make out a letter or series of them in a word, I guessed at the correct spelling and used that. I did not use "sic" to indicate I was following her usage/spelling, primarily because there would have been too many of them. If, at any point I could not make out a word or series of them due to spelling or the faint writing I put what I thought was the correct word(s) between parentheses. In only one place was I unable to make sense of what was written, here I just used a series of dashes in the parentheses. It is interesting to note that her vocabulary was quite extensive and there were a couple of places she sent me to the dictionary to check on a word's meaning or spelling only to find she had used and spelled it correctly.

Finally, from time to time I felt the need to clarify entries or add comments using information she supplied during her lifetime or stories told by siblings and their kin. This is done by the means of brackets. The words inside those are mine, not Catharine's.

Acknowledgements

I cannot thank my cousin Paul Snyder—Ray's youngest son and 7 years my senior—enough for all the help he has given me on this project. First, through his genealogical work the family tree has been traced back to Germany and forward to the current generation with side trips down other branches. Without this information I would never have known where my mother's roots lay. Second, he has read the transcription of her diary and, because he knows the family and the area so well, was able to identify most of the family and characters that appear in it whom I didn't know. Without this information many people and places would be poorly spelled, meaningless names. Finally, because he is the last of his generation of Leonard and Irene's grandchildren still living in the area, once I started writing I have peppered him with questions about geographic as well as family history on a need-to-know-fast basis. He has been more than generous in answering each one, providing me with new information, sharing old photos and giving me a tour of Pine Grove home sites. It is safe to say that, without Paul's help none of this would have happened.

Additionally, his sister, Mary Lou Snyder Wickham, shared some of her collection of photos with me. Some are included.

Likewise, as with all my writing, I have my wife, Karen, to thank for reading, correcting and setting me straight on usage. I'd be lost without this help. If there are any errors in usage, punctuation, or spelling it is because I can never leave a manuscript alone and have inserted things after she proofed it.

As far as the story of Jeremiah and Elias Snyder's Revolutionary capture as well as some of the information on Martin I have relied on Alf Evers, <u>The Catskills, From Wilderness to Woodstock.</u> There is a complete chapter dealing with the Snyder's. Additionally, Reverend Charles Rockwell's <u>The Catskill Mountains and the Region Around</u> has an extensive section in Chapter 5 about the Snyder capture. This book, c1867, while out of print, is available at www.catskillarchives. com. Finally two other of Evers' books, <u>Woodstock, History of an American Town</u> and <u>Kingston, City on the Hudson</u> along with the one cited above have a great deal of background information about the part of the Hudson Valley and Catskills where Catharine grew up.

For information about New Amsterdam, the best book out there is Russell Shorto's <u>Island in the Center of the World, The Epic of Dutch Manhattan and the Forgotten Colony That Shaped America</u>. Don't be put off by the length of the title; it is an excellent, well written book on the settlement of the Dutch colony up until the British took control.

Finally there is a lot of Palatine information to be found on The Olive Tree Genealogy site at www.rootsweb.com including links to passenger lists of the ships that brought them to America. There is also a Wikipedia site for the Palatines if one wants a quick byte of information about them. For anyone with Palatine ancestors or who needs to know information, there is an organization that you can join—Palatines to America—German Genealogy Society whose NY chapter is headquartered in New Windsor, NY. Your best bet is to go to the national society's homepage at www.palam.org. The Society offers a lot of information in the form of books and research about these people. I also leaned on Walter Allen Knittle's <u>Early Eighteen Century Palatine Emigration</u> for information about their resettlement in both Ireland and North America.

Catharine's Diary

Wednesday January 1, 1919: This is the first I ever wrote in a diary. Orpha Bishop gave it to me for Christmas. I am sick in bed with the "flu". [The use of the quotation marks is Catharine's. This was 1919 and the world was in the midst of the "Spanish Flu" pandemic but, since her particular illness was short lived and, certainly not fatal, I doubt that it was this variety of flu. Interestingly as well, in the whole of this diary, this is the only reference to any type of flu so it would seem the family was not touched by this epidemic.]

Thursday Jan. 2: Am in bed yet today but feel some better. Rec'd a postal from Mamie [no idea] today and a letter from Aunt Esther of which I was glad for.

Friday Jan 3: The Dr. came today said my temperature was normal and says I can get up Sunday. So I am so happy and I am to have a baked potato and poached egg tomorrow.

Saturday Jan 4: Well I am getting along fine feel much better today and find it hard to stay in bed. I have my doll in bed with me and I am looking at some pictures.

Sunday Jan 5: I am sitting up today for the first feel fine. Aunt Esther and Harry was here today. Came up on train and drove from Saugerties up. Going with sleighs today for the first this year.

Monday Jan 6: A nice sunshiny day today. Lizzie washed today. Was down stairs today for dinner for the first. Wish I could go out and ride down hill. Aunt Kate, Irving and Uncle Dewitt was up for a few minutes today.

Tuesday Jan 7: Rec'd a roll of pictures to cut out from Lydia Russell today. Arthur and Evadora went over to Russell's today. It's quite a nice day today.

Wednesday Jan 8: It is a nice day today it snowed a little this a.m. but the sun is out now. Pa went to Saugerties today. The Grocery man here today. I went outdoors today for the first. I rec'd a letter from Orpha tonight.

Thursday Jan 9: Fair today. Rec'd a big package from Orpha and her sister today nuts, crackers, 6 grapefruit and dozen oranges 3 boxes and 2 rolls of candy. Uncle Char. was up this p.m. and they played dominoes.

Friday Jan 10: Real cold day today. Was out for a sleigh ride this a.m. Lizzie went to Saugerties with horse and sleigh this p.m. Today is Ma's birthday. She is 56 years old.

Saturday Jan 11: It a nice day today only very cold. Ray drawed over corn stalks today and went after a load of saw dust.

Sunday Jan 12: It is a nice day today. Lizzie and Ray went to church this a.m. and from there they are going to Helen Kiersted. Pa went down to Mr. Bishop's this p.m.

Monday Jan 13: Mother and Lizzie washed today. Lizzie just down with the mail. Ray went to village this p.m. Mother is making me a new dress. I have been crocheting on a new yoke. Must get to bed now. Ray and Liz were down to Uncle Char.

Tuesday Jan 14: It is quite a nice day today. Pa went to Saugerties this p.m. I have crocheted some on my yoke today. Mother has my dress nearly done. The snow is melting fast.

Wednesday Jan 15: It was quite a nice day today. Lizzie took my picture today with the dog. [The dog's name was Carlo, a collie/shepherd mix and was the only pet Catharine had growing up. Apparently a couple of years later he was hit by a car and killed. Unfortunately these particular photos have been lost but there are several others, none of which appear to have been taken in January. One of these is used on the front cover; the other with Dot Merkle is included with photos at the end.] Lizzie made some molasses candy today. Mamma finished my dress and it is lovely.

Thursday Jan. 16: It was a nice day today. Mother and I went to Kingston today p.m. to Aunt Esther now. Lizzie took us to Saugerties and brought us back up to the depot.

Friday Jan. 17: It rained a little today. Ma had her skirt fixed today. Mrs. Wicks fixed it for her. And in the afternoon Ma and I went up to Jennie's [probably a cousin of Irene's] and at supper Aunt Esther came up and we went to the movies they were great.

Saturday Jan 18: It was quite a nice day today. Mother and I went uptown this a.m. and we got a new coat. Mine a green coat. It cost $7.97. Mother's is black with brown plush around the collar and cuffs. They had to be fixed over so they were to send them down tonight but they haven't come yet.

Sunday Jan 19: We went with Aunt Sarah to her church this a.m. The text St. John's 4th Chap. 3rd v. and in the p.m. we went to see pictures in the same church and at night went to a memorial service on Clinton Ave.

Monday Jan. 20: A fine day today. Ma and I spent the day with Aunt Sarah. Mother got some lace curtains for stairs tonight. Finished my yoke today.

Tuesday Jan 21: It was quite a nice day today. Mother and I came home today. Lizzie was at station to meet us. Pa and Lizzie like our coats very much.

Wednesday Jan 22: It was a nice day today. I went along with Pa to the mail box to get the mail. And rec'd a letter and bunch of papers from Dot.

Thursday Jan. 23: A warm nasty day today began to rain towards night. Pa went down after the mail and Aunt Janey sent some funny papers up to me.

Friday Jan 24: Pa and I went to Saugerties today and took a music lesson the first since I had the "Flu" and she game me Moon Winks for a lesson. [Catharine played the piano often once she became an adult, especially for Sunday school. Lack of practice combined with a severe hearing loss probably prevented her from playing well as she got older. However, one of her most precious possessions was a Wurlitzer electric organ her husband gave her in the late 1960's that she played often.] We have new neighbors, Mr. and Mrs. Rector. They called this p.m.

Saturday Jan 25: It was a fine winter's day today. Lizzie went to Mr. Russell's after Ray this p.m. I held the horse while put a neverslip in. [This was a patented, steel, self-sharpening horse shoe used, primarily, to prevent carriage and trotting/pacing horses from slipping in mud or on ice.] I finished lace enough for Ma's corset cover this p.m.

Sunday Jan 26: It was a nice day today. This p.m. Ray, Ma and I went down to Merkel's and took Ethel [actually Ethel Mae Croswell who married a Snyder outside the immediate family] her new dress. They were all pretty well.

Monday Jan 27: A nice day today. I started to school again the first since I was sick. Liz and Ray up to Ida's tonight. And Uncle Char. and Aunt Janey was up here. We played dominoes and had ice cream.

Tuesday Jan 28: A nice warm day. I was to school. Mother and Liz went down to Aunt Kate's and Addie came along home. Uncle Meyer's folks down a little while in the evening.

Wednesday Jan 29: A nice day today. Lizzie went with a train this a.m. to Atlantic City. I was to school. Addie still here.

Thursday Jan. 30: I was to school a nice day. Pa took Addie down to Aunt Kate's this p.m. then came around and fetched me home from school.

Friday Jan. 31: It was a nice day today. I was to school. We made a hat for Washington's Birthday. We rec'd a card from Lizzie today she arrived safe.

Saturday, February. 1: Fair but windy today. Was to Saugerties to my music lesson. She give me part of Moon Wink's to memorize.

Sunday Feb 2: Quite cold and windy. Ray, Ma and I was us to church this a.m. The text Eph. 13th ,6th. Gave me a piece to speak for missions.

Monday Feb 3: It was a nice day today. Pa took me to school this a.m. and got a ride with Mr. Sheltise tonight so didn't walk either way. Ma washed and ironed today. Ray and Liz got their letters for to go to Mohonk [A resort in the Catskills where Orpha, Liz and Ray worked. The story is that it was here that Ray met Orpha. The hotel still exists.] this summer.

Tuesday Feb 4: It was a nice day today. Pa took me to school today. I went up and got the milk tonight.

Wednesday Feb 5: A nice day today. Pa took me to school. The groceryman was up to day.

Thursday Feb 6: It was a nice day today. I was to school. We rec'd a letter from Lizzie today. I wrote her a letter tonight.

Friday Feb 7: A nice day was to school. Rec'd a folder from Lizzie today. Pop got a load of hay from Russell's today.

Saturday Feb 8: It was cloudy day today. I picked a quart of wintergreen berries today. Sent a box full to Lizzie.

Sunday Feb 9: A nice day to day. Mother and Ray was to church. I've got another piece to speak for church. Uncle Char. was up here this p.m.

Monday Feb 10: Another cold day to day. Was to school. Mother washed and ironed.

Tuesday Feb. 11: A nice day. Was to school. Pa came after me tonight. Lizzie sent me a card today.

Wednesday Feb. 12: It was a nice day today. Was no school, Lincoln's Birthday. Well guess I will crawl in.

Thursday Feb 13: A nice day Pop went to Saugerties. No school, teacher went to tend some meeting. We called up to Uncle Meyer's a little while tonight.

Friday Feb 14: A rainy day today. Wasn't to school. Uncle Char. was up here a little while this p.m. Rec'd a valentine from Lizzie and the Merkles.

Saturday Feb 15: A cloudy day today. Pa and I was to Saugerties. I took my music lesson. Got a new piece to play.

Sunday Feb 16: A windy day today. Pa and I was up to Uncle Meyer's this p.m. Albert's folks after, we had ice cream. And we all went down to Uncle Char. tonight for supper. Had ice cream there also. Ray walked up to the Overlook House [another resort on the mountain behind Woodstock, no longer in existence.] this p.m.

Monday Feb 17: A nice day today. Pa took me to school this a.m. Ma washed and ironed today. We rec'd a letter from Aunt Esther and Jennie today.

Tuesday Feb 18: A windy day today. Pa took me to school this a.m. and come after me tonight. Rec'd a valentine from Crawford and Dot today. Floyd Burton was down here a little while tonight. We played dominoes.

Wednesday Feb 19: A nice day today. Was to school. The grocerman was here today. Ray rec'd a letter from Lizzie today, she has a cold.

Thursday Feb 20: A nice day today. Ray and mother went to Saugerties today to get Ernie a new suit. I rode along with them to school.

Friday Feb 21: Went to school today. Started snowing. Pa came after me. Arthur came home on the train tonight. Ray went down to meet him.

Saturday Feb 22: A nice day today. Ray took Arthur over to Hurley tonight. Pa up to Uncle Meyer's. Ground covered with snow yet not enough for sleighing.

Sunday Feb 23: It rained a little this a.m. but cleared off so we went to church, Foreign mission Sunday. I spoke my piece. Uncle Meyer was down here a little while tonight.

Monday Feb 24: A nice day today. Pa took me and came for me at school. Ma washed and ironed today.

Tuesday Feb 25: This is what I got for my birthday: 3 pairs of stockings, a hair receiver and a bottle of cologne, a box of writing paper and 5 cards and a cake with 10 candles.

Wednesday Feb 26: A nice day today. Pa took me to school. Rec'd a birthday card from Mabel saying if I would tell her the name and no. of my book would forward it. And a B.card from Liz too said she had sent me a box of candy.

Thursday Feb 27: A nice day today. Was to school today. Rec'd my box of candy from Lizzie they are delicious.

Friday Feb 28: Rained a little towards night. Was to school. Rode up with Uncle Raymond, Adline and Uncle Chester. Was down this p.m. Adline stayed all night.

Saturday March 1: A nice day today. Went to Saugerties took my music lesson got book 3 and another piece to play. 10 for both. We rec'd a letter from Maude, her baby not very well.

Sunday Mar 2: A nice day today. Ray and Adline went to church. We stayed home thinking Albert's folks might come but they didn't.

Monday Mar 3: A nice day today. Was to school. Pa tapped one little maple tree today and he gathered 3 water pails full.

Tuesday Mar 4: A nice day today. Was to school. We boiled down our sap today had a little over a quart. Took the mail up to Uncle Meyer's tonight.

Wednesday Mar 5: A nice day today. Was to school. Pa, Ma and Adline was to aunt Mary's today. We rec'd a letter from Luther today. The groceryman was up today.

Thursday Mar 6: Quite a nice day today but a little colder. Pa took me to school today. Floyd was down a little while tonight. We played dominoes, Pa & I beat.

Friday Mar 7: A nice day today. Pa fetch me from school tonight. Adline went down to Uncle Char. tonight.

Saturday Mar 8: A nice day today. This a.m. when Pa went out to the barn there was a little calf. She is just like her mother. I beat Pa 6 games of dominoes today.

Sunday Mar 9: A rainy day today. Pa, Ma and I went down to Uncle Will's a little while today & when we came back Ray wasn't home. It was Irving Croswell's birthday today.

Monday Mar 10: A nice day today. Rode down with Mr. Sheltise this a.m. & Ray came after me a little ways tonight. We rec'd a big package from Dora MacNaught [a cousin, her husband, Frank, was Business Manager at the Woods Hole Marine Biological Laboratory from 1913 until 1949], 3 dresses for me & a pair of slippers & some pictures.

Tuesday Mar 11: A nice day today. Walked both ways to school. Ray & Uncle Meyer went to Kingston. Uncle Meyer traded his horse and got a new one. It was Ethel Snyder's birthday today.

Wednesday Mar. 12: A nice day today. Pa and Ray went over to Russell's and got a load of hay.

Thursday Mar. 13: A nice day today. There was no school teachers' conference. We rec'd a letter from Lizzie today. She is well.

Friday Mar 14: A nice day today. Was to school. Uncle Chester was down here a little while p.m. Ray went to Saugerties and he went around by Maude's & took some things.

Saturday Mar 15: A nice but cold day today. Pa & I went to Saugerties. I took my music lesson. Pa got me a new pair of shoes. We rec'd a letter from Evadora today, they are well.

Sunday Mar 16: A rainy day today. Pa went down to Uncle Char. and Ray went up to Uncle Meyers. Floyd Burton was down a little while this p.m. I wrote a letter to Lizzie.

Monday Mar. 17: A rainy day today. Ray took and got me from school today. Mother washed but didn't hang up her clothes. Ray bought a wagon of Hasve(?) Cole today. [I couldn't decipher this sequence but suspect it may have been some kind of fuel although Catharine surely knew the difference between the spelling of coal and cole.]

Tuesday Mar 18: Cleared off and warmer today. I rode both ways to school. Uncle Chester was down after the mail this p.m. We rec'd a letter from Arthur, they are both well.

Wednesday Mar 19: A windy day today. Was to school. Ray went up to the shop this a.m. The grocerman was here today.

Thursday Mar 20: A nice day today. I was to school. The new neighbor came by today and they brought me a box of candy and a wash tub & wash board.

Friday Mar 21: A nice day today. Was to school. Ray cleaned the yard and layed board walks. Ray went to a party to Cousin's tonight. Mr. Cousin [a neighbor] has sold his place.

Saturday Mar. 22: A nice day today. Wind blows a gale. Ray went with Mr. Sheltise to Katsbaan today. [A town north and west of Saugerties near where Martin's farmstead was located, his initials are in the original cement of the Dutch Reformed Church there and he was probably one of the founding members. Also near the site of "Woodstock".] Pa went to Saugerties this p.m.

Sunday Mar 23: A nice day today. Ray and I was to Church. The text was 16 Chap and 8th & 9th of Luke. Alberts visited here today.

Monday Mar 24: A nice day today. Went to school. Rode down with Mr. Sheltise. Ma washed and ironed.

Tuesday Mar 25: A nice day today. Was to school. Rode with Mr. Sheltise. The harness broke and horse kicked throwed us out and hurt Mr. Sheltise.

Wednesday Mar 26: A nice day today. Was to school. Pa's working with Uncle Dewett and so Ma went to see Aunt Kate today.

Thursday Mar. 27: Was to school today rained towards night so stopped in to Aunt Janey's a little while. We rec'd a letter from Elizabeth today she is well.

Friday Mar 28: There was no school today. An awful wind & snow storm today, blowed and broke a window in, glass all over the floor.

Uncle Wills auction was today and Ray went to it & blowed so before he got home. Ray lost his hat.

Saturday Mar 29: Cold windy and snow blowing today. Ray popped some corn today. Down in the woods trees blowed across the road & Ray had to go get Peter to cut them out.

Sunday Mar 30: A nice day today. We made some ice cream today. Ray and Pop went to Uncles Wills to get a window in place of the one that blowed out and did all clocks ahead an hour today.

Monday Mar. 31: A nice day today. I was to school. We started with one new teacher today, his name Mr. Fitzgerald. I like him very much. Mr. Sheltise came home today but he can't move his arm very much.

Tuesday April 1: A nice but cold day today. There was no school on account of the parade for the boys in Kingston. Uncle Chester came down today to putty the windows. Mrs. Richter took Anna's and my picture today.

Wednesday Apr. 2: A nice day today. Was to school. Ma and Mrs. Richter went away today. Ray moved Mr. Sheltise today to where he is going to live. Uncle Chester did not work at the windows today.

Thursday Apr 3: A nice day today. Walked both ways to school. Uncle Chester is working at the windows today. I rec'd my book from Mabel Merkle for my birthday and a hander kerchief also.

Friday Apr. 4: A nice day today. Uncle Chester worked at the windows. Aunt Katherine & Anna was down this p.m. after the mail.

Saturday Apr. 5: A nice day today. Pa and I was to Saugerties today. I took my music lesson. I got a new piece "Orange Blossoms". Think I will like it. Arthur and Evadora came home tonight.

Sunday Apr. 6: A nice day today. Arthur & Evadiora and I were out picking trailing arbutus. We found a few. Arthur & Evadora went over to Russell's to night Aunt Janey & Uncle Char. were up a little while this p.m.

Monday Apr. 7: A warm day today. I was to school. The butcher was here after the calf it weighed 158 lb. Uncle Chester started painting the windows this p.m. Ma washed and ironed & put her lettuce seed in the ground.

Tuesday Apr 8: A nice warm day today. There was no school, teachers went to conference. Pa & Ma went to Saugerties. Pa got a new suit. Uncle Chester painted the windows today.

Wednesday Apr. 9: Not quite so warm today. I went to school. Ray & Uncle Char. worked on the road today. Ray went up to Woodstock tonight to a supper. Lots of wild geese went north today.

Thursday Apr. 10: A nice day today. I was to school. Ray dug some horseradish tonight and we ground it up. And Aunt Katherine & her sister and little Anna was down a little while this evening.

Friday Apr. 11: A rainy day today. Ray took me to school. Ray sent Liz some trailing arbutus and Pop sent her a cake of maple sugar.

Saturday Apr. 12: A nice day today. Pop went to Saugerties this afternoon. Uncle Ches. was down this a.m. but did work at the windows. Ray worked on the road today and stayed down at Uncles Char for his dinner.

Sunday Apr. 13: A nice day today. Ray and Mother was to church. Pa & I stayed home and got dinner. Uncle Char. was up a little while this p.m.

Monday Apr 14: A nice day today. I was to school. Rec'd a Package from Dot some eats from her birthday party. Marion[no idea] came up yesterday for her Easter vacation.

Tuesday Apr. 15: A nice day today. I was to school. Floyd Burton was down a little while tonight. We played dominoes. Pa & I beat. Uncle Chester painted the windows today. Ray worked on the road today.

Wednesday Apr. 16: Rained all day today. Ray took me both ways to school. And he went to Saugerties this a.m. Ma cleaned the storeroom today.

Thursday Apr. 17: A nasty, cloudy day today and rained towards night. I was to school today & rec'd a Easter package from Lizzie but don't dare open it until Easter. Ma cleaned the south room today.

Friday Apr. 18: A nice day today. I was to school. Have a terrible cold and sore throat. We rec'd a letter from Ernie today, he's well.

Saturday Apr. 19: A nice day today. Pa and I went to Saugerties. I took my music lesson. Aunt Esther came to our house this a.m. I opened my Easter package from Elizabeth. She was fine.

Sunday Apr. 20: A nice day today. We were all to church except Pa, he stayed home. Ray joined the church today and 2 other boys. Ernie was up a little while today. Aunt Esther went home tonight.

Monday Apr. 21: A nice day today. I was to school. Mr. Cousin had his auction today. I was down a little while after school tonight.

Tuesday Apr. 22: A nice day today. I was to school. Pa went to the village today and went around by Aunt Kate's and brought Adline back with him.

Wednesday Apr. 23: A nice day today. I was to school. Adline is here yet. Ma and her cleaned the north room today.

Thursday Apr. 24: A rainy day today. I was to school. Mother and Pa was to Saugerties today and I rode down with them. Aunt Janey had the Dr. today she has quinsy sore throat.

Friday Apr. 25: A cold snowy day. I was to school. Mother was down to Aunt Janey's a little while today and she is better. Ray sent off for some little chickens and they came today alright.

Saturday Apr. 26: A cold day today. Pa was to burying ground meeting. Mother and Adline cleaned the parlor today. Adline still here.

Sunday Apr. 27: A nice day today. Adline and Ray and I went to church. Pa went down to Uncle Char. Aunt Jane is better. Uncle Chester and Peter Snyder was here a little while this p.m.

Monday Apr. 28: A cloudy, rainy day today. I was to school. Mother and Adline cleaned the cellar today but did not wash.

Tuesday Apr. 29: A windy day today. I was to school. Adline and Mother wash and ironed today. Mr. S was here a little while this p.m.

Wednesday Apr. 30: A nice day today. I was to school. Adline and Mother cleaned the bedroom and buttery today. [The buttery was probably located in the lower part of the house where it was built into the hill. It was here the family stored those things they wanted to keep cool.]

Thursday May 1: A cloudy day and rained tonight. I was to school. Mother and Adline finished the room today. Rec'd a letter from Liz and Luther. Liz has been having a time with cold.

Friday May 2: A nice day today. I went to school this a.m. and teacher said it was Arbor Day so played some games and came home. Rec'd a letter from Aunt Esther tonight.

Saturday May 3: A nice day today. Pa, Mother and I went to Saugerties. I took my music lesson. Adline cleaned the stoop today. We rec'd a letter from Arthur and Evadora today.

Sunday May 4: A lovely day today. There was no church. Danley[I assume this was the minister] on a vacation. Mr. & Mrs. Richters took Mother and I out for auto ride this a.m. Took us to Saugerties & then to Kingston around by West Hurley and Woodstock and home, dandy ride.

Monday May 5: Nice and clear this morning but rained towards night. I was to school. Pa draw out manure today. Mother and Adline cleaned the kitchen today. Mrs. Richter gave me a cents box. I picked some violets.

Tuesday May 6: A nice day today. I was to school. Adline and Mother washed and ironed. Took the milk up to Mr. Richters tonight. Uncle Raym and Uncle Meyer and Uncle Char are scraping the road today. [There were no highway crews in 1919, you were responsible for the road that was on your property.]

Wednesday May 7: A rainy day today. There was no school today, teacher's conference. Mother set out her flowers today. We rec'd letters from Aunt Esther, Ernie and Maude. Maude has moved.

Thursday May 8: A nice day today. I was to school. Merlin[apparently a neighbor who had a phone.] came up with a telephone message from Maude. Her baby is dead, he is six months all the 19th of this month. [This would have been George, the second of Maude's children to die as an infant.]

Friday May 9: A rainy day today. I did not go to school, stayed home to go to the funeral but so rainy did not go. Ray and Mother went.

Saturday May 10: A rainy day today. Pop took Mother down to depot this a.m. She is going to Buffalo to Luther's. He is going to meet her at Albany and go with her from there on. Adline is going to keep house for us.

Sunday May 11: A nasty cold day today. No one went to church. Mother's Day up to our church today. Uncle Char. was up a little while this p.m. Uncle Meyer was down tonight. Anna is sick.

Monday May 12: A rainy day today. I was to school. It was Pa's birthday, he is 60 years old. Adline washed but did not hang up her clothes so rainy. Pa drawed some manure out.

Tuesday May 13: A nice warm day today. I was to school. We didn't get nothing from Mother today yet. Pa finished drawing out manure today.

Wednesday May 14: A nice warm day today. I was to school. Got a ride up with Mr. Richter. Also got a letter from Mother. She got there alright. Luther has an auto. She has been out riding in it. Pa doesn't feel very good. [This apparently is when Leonard's mental health started to decline as it is her first mention of it.]

Thursday May 15: It rained a little tonight. I was to school. Got a letter in it and a dollar bill for my music, think it just grand. Pa don't feel any better today.

Friday May 16: A nice day today. I was to school. Pa is the same way. I mailed 12 letters this a.m. for Richters. Aunt Katherine and Mrs. Richter was down after the mail this p.m.

Saturday May 17: A rainy day today. Raymond rec'd a letter from Mother, she is well and I rec'd a letter from Evadora also, they are all well.

Sunday May 18: A lovely day today. Ray and I was to church. Adline stayed home to get dinner. We had lettuce today. Peter lost a fat calf down in the woods, it ran away.

Monday May 19: A nice day today. I went down to school but there wasn't any so came back. And Mrs. Richter and Mr. Richter were going to the village so took me along in there auto.

Tuesday May 20: A cloudy day today. I went to school. Pop put twine over the potato patch. Adline ironed today. Ray worked down to Cadwell's [local farmer that employed Ray] today. They got 3 more cows today.

Wednesday May 21: A rainy day today. I went to school. Uncle Char. was up here a little while and Aunt Katherine and Anna was down also. Groceryman was here.

Thursday May 22: A rainy day today. I didn't go to school. Uncle Meyer and Mrs. Richter were down to our house today. Pop's sick.

Friday May 23: A nice day today. I was to school. Another little girl came to school today. Pa went down to Aunt Janey's this p.m. to get shaved. Doesn't feel good. I rec'd a letter from Aunt Esther and Ernie.

Saturday May 24: A cloudy day today. Took my music lesson. Richters took Pop and I down to village and brought us back. Pop went to Dr. I rec'd a letter from Mother. Said she didn't think she would come home til May 31st.

Sunday May 25: A nice day today. Ray and Adline went to church. I went along with Ray down to see his cows he milks down were he works. Richters took Uncle Ches and Uncle Raymond around the dam today. Richters and Uncle Meyer and Aunt Katherine & Anna were down a little while tonight.

Monday May 26: A nice day today. I was to school. Uncle Ches was down a little while this p.m. Pa doesn't feel good. Was up to Uncle Meyer's this p.m.

Tuesday May 27: A nice day today. I was to school. Aunt Katherine and Mrs. Richter were down after the mail this p.m. Pa has been so sick today. He worries over everything. I got a postal from Mother and Elizabeth today, they are all well.

Wednesday May 28: A nice day today. I was to school. Pa doesn't feel good at all today. Mr. Richter went to Saugerties tonight. They wanted me to go along but have to watch the chickens.

Thursday May 29: A nice but warm day today. I was to school. Got a postal from Aunt Esther today and one from Elizabeth. She sent her and Orpha's pictures. Pa doesn't feel good at all today. Art and Evadora came home tonight.

Friday May 30: A nice day today. Ray, Adline, Evadore and I were to festival today. Art stayed home with Pop. I marched into the parade and so did Ray. [I assume this was either Saugerties's or Woodstock's Memorial Day Parade.] Art and Evadora went over to Russell's tonight.

Saturday May 31: A nice day today. Art and Eva came back today. I washed off the porch today and helped Adline with the work. Art and Pop went to village today. Pop went to Dr. got a lot of medicine. Ray went out fishing tonight with Burtons.

Sunday June 1: A nice day today. Mother came home. Art and I went down to meet her. Lute came along with her. Lute went back tonight. Art and Eva went too. Cora Snyder sent me a music book. Cora [probably a misprint, she meant Orpha] Bishop was to see me a little while today. Ray came home this a.m. from fishing had 4 trout and 4 eels but was some sleepy, been up all night.. [In those days they were more likely to "fish" with nets and eelpots than hook and line—this wasn't recreational fishing.]

Monday June 2: A hot day today. I was to school. We made the garden tonight. The little boy up to Richter's was down to see me a long while tonight. Adline went down to Aunt Janey's tonight.

Tuesday June 3: A terrible hot day thought I would melt coming home from school, so hot. I got a letter from Dot today. Adline is going down to Aunt Janey's to stay a little while tonight. Uncle Char. went to be jury and Aunt J is alone.

Wednesday June 4: Uncle Char came home, didn't need him to be juryman until next Monday. A hot day today. I was to school. Pa did not feel good at all today. He worries over everything. The groceryman was here today.

Thursday June 5: A warm day today. I was to school. Pa the same today. The little boy up to Mrs. Richter's was down to see me and his father and mother and brother came up there last night.

Friday June 6: A nice day today, rained a little towards night. I came home from school bare footed had a blister on my heel. Pa feels just the same.

Saturday June 7: A rainy day today. Pa, Ma and I went to Saugerties. I took my music lesson. We got caught in a shower and went under a shed, didn't get bad wet. Pa the same today.

Sunday June 8: A rainy day today. Ray had to work today so no one went to church. I wrote to Dorthea and Elizabeth. Was up to the Richter's an hour this p.m. Pa gets spells he hollers right out and gets so crazy.

Monday June 9: A rainy day today. I was to school. Pop the same today. Mother washed today.

Tuesday June 10: A lovely day today. Rode both ways to school. I heard today that Aunt Joan is dead, died Monday a.m. Mother picked enough strawberries for supper tonight.

Wednesday June 11: A nice day today. Pop and Mother was to Aunt Joan's funeral. Pop no better. I was to school. We are having exams down to school.

Thursday June 12: A lovely day today. I was to school. We had some more exams today. I didn't pass in Geography and Arithmetic. Uncle Ches. was down this p.m.

Friday June 13: A nice day today. I was to school. Today is the last day of school. I got a chart and the teacher's picture.

Saturday June 14: A nice day today, had a little shower. I slept a long while this p.m. Mother and I was up to Mrs. Richter's tonight.

Sunday June 15: A rainy day today. Mother and Ray went to church. I stayed home and got the dinner. Uncle Char. was up a little while this p.m.

Monday June 16: A nice day today. I picked enough strawberries for Ray's dinner today. The groceryman was here today. Pa the same, was down to Uncle Char. this p.m.

Tuesday June 17: A nice day today. I picked enough strawberries for Ray's dinner today. I help Pa when he cultivated. I went behind and fixed the hills he knocked down. Got a letter from Dot was to Munny's[no idea what this was as it is written in the margin and smudged].

Wednesday June 18: A nice day today. Mother doesn't feel well today has such a headache and such pain in her side. Pa the same. Uncle Chester was down this a.m.

Thursday June 19: A lovely day today. Richters took me for a long auto ride today. We went down to see the circus but there wasn't enough people to have any so then they took me for a long ride.

Friday June 20: A rainy day today. I hoed some corn today and picked a few currants and strawberries. Pa is the same way, cultivated a little in the corn today. Mother the same way doesn't feel very well.

Saturday June 21: A nice day today. I was to Saugerties, took my music lesson. We expected my music teacher up today but couldn't come. Pa was to Dr., the same old way. Mother killed a big muskrat today.

Sunday June 22: A nice day today. Ray had to work this Sunday again so no one went to church. Uncle Frank came up this a.m. and stayed until this p.m. Pa the same old way.

Monday June 23: A nice day today. This a.m. when we got up all the little chickens out back of the barn were dead, something had come and killed them in the night and took 11 away and left. We set traps tonight to catch the animal.

Tuesday June 24: A nice day today. This a.m. there was nothing in the traps but Ray shot a great big black and white skunk. Think that must have been the chicken killer. Set traps again tonight.

Wednesday June 25: A nice day today. Didn't catch anything in the traps we set. I was up to Uncle Meyer's a little while this p.m. Pa is about the same way. Groceryman was here today. Ma was down also.

Thursday June 26: A terrible rainy day today. Mr. Richter and Uncle Chester was down a little while this p.m. Pa the same old way. Mother cleaned upstairs and down today.

Friday June 27: A rainy day today. Uncle Char. was up this p.m. I sewed six blocks today [apparently she was making a quilt]. Pa the same way. Mrs. Richter was down a little while tonight.

Saturday June 28: A nice day today. Richters took me down to Saugerties in the car and got me a dish of ice cream. Pa the same way.

Sunday June 29: A nice day today. Ray and I and Mother was to church. We expected Mr. Fredrick to preach but he didn't get there to preach. In the p.m. Richters took Pop, Ray and I in their auto. We went to see Mr. Sheltise and then back to where Ray works and then to Woodstock and back.

Monday June 30: A nice day today. Mother and I washed today. We also picked some currants. We rec'd a letter from Cora, they are real well. Mrs. Richter game me 20 cents tonight for carrying up the milk.

Tuesday July 1: A nice day today. Pa, Ma and I were to Saugerties. I took my music lesson. I got one hard piece. We got a letter from Aunt Esther today. Pa was to Dr., said he was better.

Wednesday July 2: A nice day today. Richters took Mother to Saugerties in their car and went over to a man by name of Mr. Derrek and got a bushel of cherries. Canned some cans tonight. [This is what she wrote; I assume they canned the cherries.]

51

Thursday July 3: A nice day today. We had 20 cans of cherries in all. Aunt Esther and Evadora and Art came up to our house tonight. Art brought me a lovely box of chocolate candies. Herman was up today, has to go back to the Navy today.

Friday July 4: A hot day today. Richters went away this a.m. Mrs. Richter gave me a lot of fireworks. We had them tonight, they were fine. I had 6 boxes of sparklers, saved them for some other nights.

Saturday July 5: A hot day today. Ray took Evadora & Arthur over to her folks tonight. Aunt Esther went along and went to see Aunt Kate a little while. I had some sparklers tonight. We had ice cream today.

Sunday July 6: A rainy day today. No one went to church. Ray had to work today. He brings 3 quarts of milk home every a.m. Pa was terrible today. We got 9 little pigs. Uncle Meyer took Aunt Esther home tonight.

Monday July 7: A nice sunshiny day today. Art came back home this a.m. Didn't go back to Newburgh, is going to help Pa with the haying. I picked a qt. of blackcaps today. Pa was same old way. Marion is down to Uncle Char. now. Ray got 13 little chicks and 2 hens today.

Tuesday July 8: A nice day today. Art cut down and is going to get some hay in tomorrow. Pop worries over everything. Uncle Meyer was down tonight. Marion and Uncle Char. came up a while tonight. Bernice Snyder was operated on today for appendicitis.

Wednesday July 9: A nice day today. Uncle Char. mowed some hay today. Pa & Art got some hay in and I rode on 2 loads. The groceryman was here today. Pop the same old way. Bernice came out of her operation alright.

Thursday July 10: A rainy day today. Art went down and the long lost box that Lute sent when she was there. There was a new suit of clothes and pair of shoes and pens and pencils and onions and basket. Pa the same. Art got 16 quarts of blackcaps tonight. Bernice the same. [She would recover, marry and have a son and a daughter.]

Friday July 11: A nice day today. We got in a lot of hay today. Art still here. I had a lot of rides. I picked 5 quarts of berries today. Pa the same way.

Saturday July 12: A nice day today. Got in some more hay today. I rode on the hay. Ma & I picked 4 qts. of berries today. Ray took Art over to Hurley tonight. Pa the same. Rec'd a box of candy from Eliz & a letter from teacher.

Sunday July 13: A nice day today. Marion and Uncle Char. was up a little while this a.m. and Fred Lewis & wife[neighbors] brought Aunt Ida & Uncle Will up in the car to see us this p.m. Pa the same.

Monday July 14: A nice day today. I went along with Ray this a.m. when he went to his work and I picked 4 qts. of blackberries and the p.m. picked 2 qts of black berries and black caps. Pa the same way. Mother washed today.

Tuesday July 15: A cloudy and rainy day today. I picked 3 qts of blackberries and red raspberries in all. Pa the same old way. We have so many berries in our swamp Pa brought a great big cluster and said they were all that way.

Wednesday July 16: A rainy day this a.m. but this p.m. it cleared up and then I picked 12 qts of blackberries. Did not go to the swamp, so wet and thought is might rain. Pa the same. Groceryman came today.

Thursday July 17: A nice day today. Richters came up today. Pa, Ma & I went to the swamp, picked 20 qts of berries some almost big as cherries. Sold 10 qts to Uncle Will this p.m., 20 cents per qt.

Friday July 18: A nice day today. I was to the swamp again today and picked 2 qts of them and 2 qts of crackers. Mrs. Richter & her uncle was down tonight brought a lot of clothes down for us.

Saturday July 19: A nice day today. Pa and I was to the village. I took my music lesson. Had 2 teeth pulled at Wygants [denist]. They kept me awake all last night so had them out. Pa was to Dr.

Sunday July 20: A nice day today. Lester, Lila and Albert was here to see Pa this p.m. Pa seems to be worse but knows if he is or isn't. Ray had to work so no one went to church.

Monday July 21: A rainy day today. Pa the same. Mother and I washed today but could not get them dry. Uncle Char. was here this a.m. Uncle Meyer was here this p.m. It was so rainy did not pick any berries today.

Tuesday July 22: A rainy day today. Mother hung up some clothes but did not get dry, had to take them down. Pa the same. Wrote to Mr. Fitzgerald today. Lester Snyder's birthday today he is 7 years old.

Wednesday July 23: A nice day today. Pa & I pick 9 qts of blackberries and near 2 qts of huckleberries for Richters. Pa better. Groceryman was here today.

Thursday July 24: A nice day today. Pa, Ma and I was to the swamp today, pick 26 qts. A lot of water in our swamp. I pick a 4 qts pail of crackers and 2 qts off swamps.

Friday July 25: A nice day today. I cleaned the porch today. Pa the same way, worries over everything. Ray has a different job, instead of working in the dairy he is working on the farm for Cadwell.

Saturday July 26: A rainy day today. Pa had the Dr. today. Dr. says he can't get well unless he goes off somewhere. He wants him to go to Art's. I did a lot of crocheting today. Pa talks about going to Art's.

Sunday July 27: A rainy day today. Richters took Ray & I around the Ashocan Dam in there auto. It was a find ride but then no on went to church. Ray has all his Sundays off now. Pa the same. Uncle Char. up.

Monday July 28: A nice day today. Ma washed. I had a terrible headache all day. Picked 3 qts of huckleberries today and nearly 2 qts of blackberries and went down to the mail box to get stamps. So many of Joe Stolls boarders down to the mail box, 8 or 10.

Tuesday July 29: A nice day today. Pa the same old way, worries over the old pig that has little pigs didn't eat her feed today and he worries over that. I guess she is only overfed and didn't feel good today.

Wednesday July 30: A nice day today. Tonight after we were all to bed the dog barked and Art called to Ray by the window to let him in. He came on the train and walked all the way. Came to take Pa back tomorrow a.m.

Thursday July 31: A nice day today. Pa went back with Art this a.m. Uncle Char took them to train. V. White [no idea, maybe a summer boarder] came to Uncle Mayer's today, staying there for a few days, called here tonight. I picked 2 qts of berries for Mrs. Richter today.

Friday August 1: A nice day today. Uncle Raymond's b'day. Ma and I picked 2 or 3 qts of berries today. We made the lettuce bed tonight. We got a yellow jacket nest in our lounge.

Saturday Aug. 2: A nice day, cool and windy day. Mother and I went down to Saugerties tonight. I didn't take my music lesson. Brought Mary [piano teacher] along back she is going to give me a lesson Monday a.m. We rec'd a letter from Eva said Pa got there alright.

Sunday Aug. 3: A nice day today. Mary, Mother, and Ray and I went to church today, Cummion [that's the way she spelled it] Sunday. I wrote a letter to Lizzie and Aunt Esther. Mary played some tonight.

Monday Aug. 4: A nice day today. I took my music lesson this a.m. Richters took Mary down this p.m. and they wanted me to go along so slipped my coat over my everyday dress & went and we went to Kingston and through the Old Senate House. Had lots of ice cream.

Tuesday Aug.5: A rainy day today. I got a folder from Pa today. Mother washed today and this p.m. we went to the swamp and just as we got our pails nearly full it started to rain so came home. Had 3 qts. Ray took a load of wood to Mr. Hyman. Ma & I was up to Mrs. Richter's tonight she gave us some things for the fair.

Wednesday Aug 6: A rainy day today. Ma baked and ironed today. Groceryman was here. We sent a box of swamp berries to Liz with him. I practiced 2 hours today on my music.

Thursday Aug 7: Cleared off this a.m. Went to the swamp this a.m. got 12 qts of swamp huckleberries. We had our fair tonight. Ray went up and Helen K---sent me a lovely brown knitting bag.

Friday Aug 8: A nice day today. We went to the swamp again today pick 13 qts. We got a letter from Art today. He is going to bring Pa home tomorrow. Didn't stay very long and Art says is no better.

Saturday Aug. 9: A nice day today. Richters went down after Art and Pop today. Pa no better. I guess I am going to go along back with Art to Newburgh. Pa got me a lovely box of candy.

Sunday Aug 10: A nice day today. I came back with Art, am to his house. Had a lovely ride. Guess I am going to stay a week. Their were people on the train that gave me lots of things to eat. Everybody all well here. Mrs. Rich is with Evadora. Must get bed made. Wrote a card to mother tonight.

Monday Aug 11: A nice day today. Mrs. Rich , Evadora, and I went to see a parade this a.m. but didn't see any. But did some shopping and I got 5 postals, sent one to Ray and one to Crawford and Dot.

Tuesday Aug 12: A nice day today. We went to Downy's park today crossed the ferry went over to Newburgh. Mrs. Rich got me a lovely pair of black stockings and Evadora got me nine hair ribbons. Was so delighted with them. Mrs. Stanforth gave me 3 little doll hats tonight also. So had a lot of things gave to me.

Wednesday Aug 13: A nice day today. Evadora and I went to the market this p.m. but most of the stores were all closed. They close every Wednesday p.m. Wrote a letter to Mother today, nothing from her yet.

Thursday Aug 14: A rainy day today. Arthur came home this a.m. didn't work today. I rec'd a letter from Mother and Lizzie today. Lizzie sent me a lovely dollar today. Wrote Helen K---- a card today and Mother and Lizzie a letter, also a card to Anna. We played dominoes. Evadora and I beat.

Friday Aug 15: Nice day this a.m. but had a shower tonight. I made a pink bag today. Mrs. Rich, I and Evadora went to Community Chautauqua today. It as fine. Some nice pieces sung by Dough Boys.

Saturday Aug 16: A nice day today but awful warm. Arthur did not have to work this p.m. so he and I went to Mt Beacon. Went up the incline. It was a fine ride and I had a fine time. Got a letter from Lydia Russell and Mother. Went with Evadora to market this a.m. Wrote a card to Aunt Esther.

Sunday Aug 17: A rainy day today. Art and Evadora and Mrs. Rich and I went to church this a.m. I went home on the 4:08 train this p.m. Mother and Pa and Mr. Richter were there to meet me. Mr. Richter took Pa and me to Cementon and West Camp and a long ride. I met Bladas on the train that used to board up to Rissys. [I'm not sure she spelled these names correctly, apparently they were just someone she met on the train. It was common for the farmers in the Catskill, including her mother and maternal grandparents, to take in summer boarders.]

Monday Aug 18: A rainy day today. Mother did not wash today. Aunt Mary spent the day here today. She is staying up to Uncle Meyer's. Pa not better he goes on terrible.

Tuesday Aug 19: Rained a little today. Mother washed today. Canned 4 cans of corn. Pa had a terrible spell today was out of his head for a while. Had to go up after Uncle Chess. Ray is going to sleep with him tonight.

Wednesday Aug 20: A nice day today. Pa, Ma and I pick beans today have a lot to pick in the corn patch yet. Pa no better. I went to swamp picked 1 qt of berries. Mother and I picked 3 qts of blackberries on Richter's tonight.

Thursday Aug. 21: A nice day today. Pa and I pick beans today have them nearly all pick. Aunt Mary was down her a little while tonight. Pa no better.

Friday Aug 22: A nice day today. I finished picking the beans tonight. Ray went down to Uncle Franks and telephoned for a Dr. I rec'd a funny paper from Lizzie today.

Saturday Aug. 23: A nice day today. Ray and I went to Saugerties tonight. I took my music lesson. Dr. said Pa was no better and he wants him to go to a hospital. Dr. telegraphed to Art to come home, so he came home tonight.

Sunday Aug 24: A nice day today. Arthur went home tonight. Ray took him down. I was down to Mary's house this p.m. Dr. was here tonight. We was going to have him take Pa to the hospital but didn't.

Monday Aug 25: A nice day today. Pa, Ma and I shelled some beans today. Aunt Jane and Uncle Char. was up tonight. Aunt Kate and Clare Spear [a neighbor] were here this p.m. for a while.

Tuesday Aug 26: A nice day today. Mother and I was to the swamp picked over 9 qts of berries. Pa no better. Mother rec'd a letter from Cora today with 3 pictures of Erwin. Also a letter from Aunt Esther and Ernie they all think ought to go to hospital.

Wednesday Aug 27: A rainy day today. We got 2 bags of beans yet to shell. Ma, Pa and I shelled today. Groceryman was here today. I took some books up to Mrs. Archer [neighbor] to read to the little boys this a.m.

Thursday Aug 28: A nice day today. Mrs. Archer and all the little boys where down here all the p.m. Mr. and Mrs. Richter took some people they knew around the Ashocan Dam and up here and back home again.

Friday Aug 29: A nice day today. Lauretta was here today, she is going to stay all night. Pa and I picked some beans today. Alfred and Harry [no idea unless these were Mrs. Archer's little boys.] were down all afternoon.

Saturday Aug 30: A nice day today. Lauretta went up to Uncle Meyer's this p.m. Mrs. Richter gave me 25 cents tonight. We finished picking beans today. Mabel, Chester, Uncle Char and Marion were up here this p.m. Marion is going back with them.

Sunday Aug 31: A nice day today. Luther came home today went back tonight. Evadora and Arthur came from Russell's today. They all think Pa ought to go to a hospital.

Monday September 1: A rainy day today. Mother, Arthur went down to see the Dr. about Pop this a.m. Had a good talk with him and brought back some medicine. Arthur and Evadora went back over to Hurley are going to take the buss from there down to Sau[gerties].

Tuesday Sept. 2: A rainy day today. Pa has been something awful today. Ray had to stay home form his work with him. Run down in the woods said he was looking for cow. Went on terrible. Uncle Meyer telephoned for Dr. to come tomorrow. Orville came up tonight is going to stay all night.

Wednesday Sept 3: A rainy day today. Well the Dr. came today and took Pa along with him to the hospitable at Kingston to try it there for a week or so. He hated to go because he had never been away from home much before. Mother washed today.

Thursday Sept 4: A nice day today. Mother ironed. Alfred and Harry where down this p.m. Ray went to his work. I washed the stoop off. I am reading a couple books. Must get to bed now.

Friday Sept 5: A nice day today. Ray telephoned to Dr. today to find out how Pop was. Said he saw him 11 o'clock last. He was a sleep then but woke him up but he was no better talked of his troubles. Alfred and Harry down a while this p.m.

Saturday Sept. 6: A nice day today. Ray, Ma and I went to the village tonight got home 11: 30. I took my music lesson. Mother seen Dr., Papa no better. Must get to bed, am terrible sleepy.

Sunday Sept 7: A nice day today. No one went to church we got of late this a.m. Ray and I went down on Caldwell's place and picked nearly a basket full of grapes. I have to get off early tomorrow morning so must get to bed.

Monday Sept. 8: A nice day today. I went to school this a.m. it started today. We have a new teacher, Miss Lawrence from Kingston looked at our books and had us write a composition and dismissed us. Got home 11:30.

Tuesday Sept. 9: A nice day today. I went to school. Like my teacher very good so far. Ray came home early tonight and said he and Mother has to go to village to see Dr, about Pa so left me with Uncle Char. Am going to stay all night.

Wednesday Sept. 10: A rainy day today. I was to school. Mother went to see Papa today. Ray took her to station on their way down met Lizzie coming so she got in and went along to see Papa too. He is no better was terrible today.

Thursday Sept. 11: A nice day today. I was to school. Like my teacher in some ways but she doesn't give hard lessons, don't think I'll learn much. She reads in the Bible, read the 23rd Psalm this a.m. [Note: there was no separation of Church and State in the Pine Grove School.] Pa no better, Dr. telephoned Ray today.

Friday Sept. 12: A nice day today. I was to school. Mother and Lizzie went to see Pa today. He is no better. Aunt Katherine and Anna were down for a while tonight. Such a windy night picked up some nuts. Teacher read 1st Psalm today.

Saturday Sept 13: A nice day today. Lizzie went down after Arthur and Evadora tonight. I wrote a letter to Dorthea today.

Sunday Sept 14: A nice day today. Mother, Ray and I went down to see Papa today. Is no better. Arthur and Evadora went to see him also and then went from there home. We went down on buss and came back on the train.

Monday Sept. 15: A nice day today. I was to school. Teacher read 121st Psalm. Lizzie and Mother canned tomatoes and chili sauce and sold $1.00 worth of them and a dozen eggs to Mrs. Bishop. Mother used the dollar for my insurance.

Tuesday Sept 16: A nice day today. I was to school. Teacher read the 24 Psalm. Pa is no better. Ray and I pick mostly a wagon box load of corn tonight down on Cadwell's place where Ray works.

Wednesday Sept 17: A nice day today. The teacher read 121st Psalm this a.m. Mother went down to Kingston this a.m. Ray, Liz and I have been picking of potatoes since 6:30 to nine. Picked over 17 bushels.

Thursday Sept 18: A nice day today. I was to school. The teacher had all say the "Lord's Prayer" today as usually, but did not read out of Bible. Lizzie went down after Mother today but she wasn't there.

Friday Sept 19: A nice day today. Lizzie went down after Mother today. I rode up with them from school. Mother came home. They took Papa to the Asylum in Middletown yesterday p.m. Teacher read 1st Psalm.

Saturday Sept. 20: A nice day today. Lizzie started to Middletown today to see Papa. Was going to stay all night to Aunt Esther's.

Sunday Sept 21: A cloudy day today. Ray, Mother and I were to church. The minister gave me a sm. Catechism today to study from. Studied the Commandments today. I slept a while this p.m. Aunt Katherine, Uncle Meyer and Anna were down a while to night.

Monday Sept 22: A rainy day today. I was to school. Teacher read the 23rd Psalm today. Lizzie came home today. Only saw Pa for a little while and stayed over night too. Arthur and Evadora went along with her.

Tuesday Sept 23: A rainy day today. I went to school. Teacher read the 1st Psalm. Lizzie went back to Atlantic City this a.m. Gave me 3 dollars to get a new hat with. Have a terrible cold.

Wednesday Sept 24: A rainy day today. I was to school today. Teacher read the Gospel of St. Matthew Chap. 5 from 1 to 7 verses. Groceryman was here today. I picked up a lot of chestnuts and walnuts [probably black walnuts] on my way home from school tonight.

Thursday Sept. 25: A nice day today. I was to school. Teacher read on in St Matthews. Ray brought home a dinner pail of nuts and mother picked quite a few under our tree.

Friday Sept 26: A nice day today. I was to school. Got a ride all the way up with Uncle Raym. Teacher read 91ˢᵗ Psalm this a.m. I must get to bed for am very sleepy.

Saturday Sept 27: A nice day today. Ray, Mother and I went to the village tonight, just got home 20 minutes of 12. I didn't take my music lesson it was too late before we got started.

Sunday Sept. 28: A nice day today. We didn't go to church we were up so late last night. I wrote a letter to Lizzie and Ernie today. Ray and I got some chestnuts tonight. Albert's folks were over a while this p.m.

Monday Sept 29: A nice day today. I was to school. Mother washed and ironed today. The teacher read the 1ˢᵗ Psalm. Ray brought home a lot of nuts tonight. He is going to work for the Masons now.

Tuesday Sept 30: A nice day today. I was to school today. Teacher read the 23ʳᵈ Psalm. Ray brought a lot of nuts again tonight. We have nearly 2 pecks of walnuts gathered.

Wednesday October 1: A rainy day today. The groceryman didn't come there was a big parade in Kingston today so likely was there. Their was no school today the teacher went to a conference.

Thursday Oct 2: A cloudy, rainy day today. I was to school. Picked quite a few chestnuts tonight on the way home. The groceryman was here today.

Friday Oct 3: A nice day today. I was to school. Teacher read 23ʳᵈ Psalm today. Lot of chestnuts again tonight and Ray brought nearly a half a bus[hel], tonight that he gathered and is gone out with some other men tonight to get some more.

Saturday Oct 4: A nice day today. Ray brought home a lot of nuts today. I didn't take my music lesson. Ray was so busy we were going to get some chestnuts in Bratt's but when Ray came up there was 2 women there thrashing trees.

Sunday Oct. 5: A nice day today. Ray, Mother and I where to church the text book Gen 2, 7th verse. Ray and I went after some chestnuts and grapes this p.m. Got enough chestnuts to send to Lizzie and a basket of wild grapes for ourselves.

Monday Oct 6: A rainy cloudy day today. I was to school. The teacher read 91st Psalm. Mother washed today but did not get clothes dry. Ray got quite a lot of nuts tonight, we have just over a bushel for ourselves now besides what Aunt Mary and Lizzie wants.

Tuesday Oct 7: A nice day today. I was to school. Teacher read the 24th Psalm today. Mother ironed today. I got a quart of nuts over at Bratts trees this p.m. Ray brought some home again tonight.

Wednesday Oct 8: A nice day today. I was to school. The teacher read the 26th Psalm today. The groceryman was here today. Ella Dubois [probably just a neighbor] was down a while this p.m. to see the groceryman.

Thursday Oct 9: A nice day today. I was to school. Teacher read parts of the 91st Psalm today. Went down on Bratts thought I might get some chestnuts but some one had been there and took them.

Friday Oct. 10: A nice day today. I was to school. Teacher read the 1st Psalm today. I rode up with Uncle Raym. tonight so didn't have to walk. Ray didn't get many nuts. Said that so many people in autos got them.

Saturday Oct. 11: A nice day today. Ray got a lot of nuts tonight. Ray, Mother and I went to Saugerties tonight. Aunt Esther came along back with us. I took my lesson. Mary gave me a new piece to play the name Bubbles.

Sunday Oct 12: A nasty gloomy day today. Ray, Mother, Aunt Esther and I all was up to Grayrock [not sure of spelling or where this is but have an inkling it may have been old Snyder homestead which is located just up Stoll Road from Leonard's.] today got over half way and couldn't get through any farther, some trees across the road so walked the rest of way. Aunt E. went back tonight. Sent a box full of nannyberries to Lizzie.

Monday Oct 13: A rainy day today. I was to school. Teacher read the 23rd Psalm. Mother washed but didn't iron. Ray didn't get many nuts tonight. Said they were pretty near all the good ones gathered.

Tuesday Oct 14: A rainy day today. I was to school. Teacher read the 24th Psalm today. Mother ironed today. I gathered a few nuts tonight. Must get to bed now am so sleepy.

Wednesday Oct 15: A rainy day today. I was to school. The teacher read the 25th Psalm. Grace S. spent the day here today. I rec'd a roll of funnies from Lizzie today. Also a letter from Pa, he is not much better.

Thursday Oct 16: A rainy day today. I was to school. Teacher read the 23rd Psalm today. I wrote a letter to Lizzie tonight. Ray went after a barrel of cider tonight.

Friday Oct 17: A nice day today. I went to school. Teacher read the 23rd Psalm. Grace and Anna was down after some cider. Ray thrashed the tree across the road on Richter's and we picked them up for them.

Saturday Oct 18: A nice day today. Ray went down after Arthur tonight. Evadora went over to her folks. Mother and I husked 8 stouts [no idea what a "stout" is unless it is some local measurement for corn] of corn this p.m.

Sunday Oct 19: A nice day today. Ray, Art, Mother and I was to church. Art went on over to Russell's is going home this p.m. Adline came up with us from church is going to help Mother clean so will be here quite a time.

Monday Oct 20: A nice day today. I was to school. Teacher read the 91st Psalm. Adline and Mother washed today. We got a letter from Mrs. Richter today doesn't say when she is coming up.

Tuesday Oct 21: A rainy day today. I was to school. Teacher read the 1st Psalm today. Ray and I shucked corn tonight. Am so sleepy so must get to bed. Have to get up early in the a.m.

Wednesday Oct 22: A nice day today. I was to school. The teacher read the 15 chapter of the Gospel of St. John. Ray and I husked corn again tonight. Groceryman was here today.

Thursday Oct 23: A cloudy day today. I was to school. The teacher read the 24th Psalm. Luther came home today. Cora and Erwin not coming till later & rode up a little ways with Uncle Raym. tonight.

Friday Oct 24: A nice day today. I was to school. Today the teacher read the 1st Psalm. I rode down with Lute and Mother they went to Saugerties this a.m. I sent Iva C. a card tonight.

Saturday Oct 25: A windy cold day today. Luther went down to Kingston on train today and brought Cora and Erwin along back. Erwin doesn't talk but walks all around and is so cute. Adline is here still.

Sunday Oct 26: A nice day today. There was no church in out church today. The minister gone away. Luther, Cora and Erin where going down to Cora's grand mother but thought they want to wait and go later. Uncle Char's cow is so sick.

Monday Oct 27: A nice day today. I was to school. Teacher read the 23rd Psalm today. Luther and Mother went to Middletown today to see Pa. Said he is terrible is out of his mind intirely in some things.

Tuesday Oct 28: A windy day today. I was to school. Teacher read the 101st Psalm today. Luther, Cora, Erwin wet home today. Ray took them down the Upilent [no idea what this word was] to see Cora's grandmother for a couple of hours. Go on the 7:03 train. Adline went down to Uncle Char's today, his cow's dead.

Wednesday Oct. 29: A nice day today. I was to school. The teacher read the 67th Psalm today. The groceryman was here today. Ella Burton was here a while this p.m.. Adline is down to Uncle Char still. Ray got 3 barrels of apples off Carles in High Woods.

Thursday Oct 30: A rainy day today. I was to school. The teacher read 1st Psalm today. Ma painted the floor today. Adline down to Uncle Char. still.

Friday Oct 31. A rainy day today. I was to school. Teacher read the 67th Psalm today. Adline came back to our house today. Ray don't get any more nuts but we have a lot of them.

Saturday November 1: A rainy day today. Ray and I were going down to Saugerties tonight but so rainy didn't. 3 weeks since I took my music lesson last.

Sunday Nov. 2: A nice day today. Ray, Mother and I went to church. Adline stayed home to get the dinner. Uncle Ches was down a while this afternoon. Haven't heard how Papa is in quite a while.

Monday Nov. 3: A nice day today. I was to school. Teacher read the 96th Psalm. Mother and Adline have been house cleaning today.

Tuesday Nov. 4: A cloudy day today. I was to school. There was school only to 12 o'clock, teacher had to go to Kingston to vote. Ray didn't work today either, drawed a lot of dirt in the garden and I and him went after a load of sawdust. A letter from Liz today and she had heard from Dr. of Pa's that he was not much better.

Wednesday Nov. 5: A nice day today. I was to school. The teacher read the 23rd Psalm. The groceryman was here today. Mother and Adline cleaned house today.

Thursday Nov. 6: A cold day today. I was to school. Teacher read the 91st Psalm today. I got out 2:30 today because I spoke a piece up to parsonage for thank offering meeting. Aunt Kate went along with us there.

Friday Nov. 7: A cold day today. I was to school. Teacher read 1st Psalm today. Adline is down to Libbie's[probably Leonard's aunt, married to William and Peter's mother]. Pete is sick, has that disease like Pop's.

Saturday Nov. 8: A nice day today. Ray and I was to Saugerties tonight. Got some honey off Marten Mower. I took a music lesson. Pete isn't much better.

Sunday Nov. 9: A cold windy day today. Ray, Mother and I where to church today. I wrote a letter to Ernie this p.m. Thought maybe Orpha Bishop and her folks might get over today but didn't come.

Monday Nov. 10: A cold windy day today. There was no school today. Ray took a load of wood to Ben Maudstock tonight. I have been pasting pictures in scrap books today. Haven't heard how Pete is today.

Tuesday Nov. 11: A rainy day today. There was no school today. Peter Snyder's quite bad with something like Papa. I have been pasting pictures in a scrap book today. [Note this was Armistice Day but, a year after the end of WWI, there is no mention of it in school, nor is it celebrated. Like the flu, it seems that WWI did not touch Pine Grove. I find this interesting.]

Wednesday Nov. 12: A rainy day today. There was school today but I didn't go, so rainy and I have a cold. And Loretta [probably Lauretta] and Uncle Meyer was down tonight and said that Lib says that Peter is terrible worse than Pa. Sent Liz a box of nuts today, grocerman with a nut cracker.

Thursday Nov. 13: A rainy day today. I didn't go to school today. I had quite a cold and Ma thought it was to rainy. I have been make more scrap books today. Peter is no better. Rec'd a letter from Pop yesterday said he was no better.

Friday Nov. 14: A nice day today. Such a short day and I had not been all week and so muddy did not go to school today. Ray got letter today from Liz saying she rec'd the box of nuts but had not got in them so has not found nut cracker.

Saturday Nov, 15: A nice day today. Ray went down for Evadora and Arthur tonight. They are coming up to help us butcher. Art was to see Pop on Thursday and he was no better.

Sunday Nov 16: A cold day today. Art, Ray, Evadora and myself went to church today, communion Sunday. Evadora and Art went over to Russell's. Ray is gone after them tonight.

Monday Nov. 17: A good butchering day today. We butchered the pigs; weighed 32.0 and 25.5 and weighed a little pig of Dr. Emerick[neighbor and local doctor] weighed 65 lbs. Art and Eva went back tonight. I was to school today. Adline came up to help butcher.

Tuesday Nov 18: A cold day today. I was to school. Teacher read 23rd Psalm. Adline here still. Peter is all right they say. Ma fried out the head cheese today. We are going to have a Thanksgiving speaking to my school tonight.

Wednesday Nov. 19: A windy day today. I was to school today. Teacher read the 1st Psalm. Adline went back to Peter's tonight. Ray butchered up to Burton's today. Pa the same I guess.

Thursday Nov. 20: A cold day today. I was to school. Teacher read the 23rd Psalm. Dr Emerick was to the school today to examine school, walked around the school house twice guess I have something of matter with my heart. [A couple of times in later life doctors though they found a murmur and she had to go through extensive tests before she had a hip replacement in her eighties. It never proved to be a problem nor could they ever establish that there was a murmur.] Mary and I swept today, teacher gave us 10 cents.

Friday Nov. 21: A cold day today. I was to school. Teacher read 91st Psalm today. Teacher gave Mary, Anna and I a piece to speak for that Thanksgiving meeting. We are not going to have it to Wednesday. Was down to Maude's tonight took some bread down.

Saturday Nov. 22: A cloudy day today. Ray. Mother, and I where to Saugerties tonight. I took my music lesson. Mary gave me a new piece to play, the name of it Evening Chimes. I love it.

Sunday Nov. 23: A cold day today. Ray, Mother and I where to church today, Luther's day, I spoke a piece, the name Raising Corn for

Massasoit. Richters came down this p.m., they are going to board here now.

Monday Nov. 24: A cold day today. I was to school. Teacher read 91st Psalm. The boys are awful in the school, the teacher don't do anything with them. The teacher isn't any good.

Tuesday Nov 25: A cold day today. I was to school. The teacher read the 23rd Psalm today. I saw Aunt Janey this a.m. and she said Uncle [I assume Charles, she doesn't say.] had see Drs. that Dr Pop [apparently this is her shorthand for the doctors that are caring for her father] and that they said they were going to change him to a room by himself where he couldn't see the actions of the other crazy people.

Wednesday Nov. 26: A rainy day today. I was to school. Teacher read the 1st Psalm. We had an entertainment to the school house this p.m., 3:20. I spoke 2, 3 pieces. Mrs. Burton was the only one there, so rainy that the people couldn't come.

Thursday Nov. 27: A sunny day today. There was no school today. Richters stayed down a while after supper tonight. We had some raisins and cider & apples. Mrs. Richter was down most all p.m.

Friday Nov. 28: A cold day today. There was no school today. We went up to Richter's to here the phonograph tonight. Stolls were there also. We had a fine time.

Saturday Nov. 29: A cold day today. I have quite a cold. Richters stayed after supper a while and played cards tonight. Rec'd a letter from Maude tonight. A big baby came to her house Sunday night name Flossie Irene. Weighed 8.0 lbs. [Flossie would not survive infancy, the third and last of Maude's children to die as an infant.] Also a letter from Arthur, Pa is saying they want us to send Pa something for Christmas.

Sunday Nov 30: Quite a warm day today. We did not go to church because Mrs. Richter wanted to go up to Mr. Burton's so started early and all of us went. Had a fine time. My cold is a little better. I wrote a letter to Liz today.

Monday December 1: A winter's day today. I did not go to school my cold was quite bad and Mother thought I would catch more cold. I don't learn much when I go to school anyhow because the teacher don't make the kids mind and the boys do everything they want too.

Tuesday Dec. 2: A cold day today. I was to school. The teacher read the 6th Psalm. We did not have school till quarter of two and then she said that we were dismissed and there would be no more school to further notice I guess. She won't teach no more, can't stand it with the boys they were awful today. My cold is better.

Wednesday Dec.3: A cold but nice day today. Mrs. Richter and I went down to the mail box this a.m. Went to see Jeb Lewis and Aunt Janice{no idea, probably some shirttail relatives, the area was full of them]. We had no mail. Think the walk did me good have quite a cough today. Groceryman was here today. Richters board here still. I have been crocheting a dish cloth for Evadora for Xmas and have it all done. Richters took us to Saugerties today also.

Thursday Dec 4: A nice but cold day today. Mr. and Mrs. Richter took Mother and I in there auto to Aunt Kate's auction. [This is another Aunt Kate, possibly a Croswell, but neither of the Aunt Kate's referred to in the Cast section. Kate was a fairly common nickname for all forms of Catharine and the family had lots of women bearing this name—Catharine was briefly called Kate in her teens. The assumption is that this Kate was selling off her farm, probably because she was widowed, but I am not sure.] Uncle Meyer bought a corn sheller for

Ray. Adline is to Aunt Kate's and she says her head and her left side feel so funny and she fell down one day. It must hurt her bad.

Friday Dec 5: A cold snowy day today. Mother cleaned today. They say we are going to hire Marjorie Cousins for teacher at school. Ray went down after the corn sheller tonight. He is going to bring corn plow along for Uncle Meyer. Rec'd word from Liz she has been to see Pop, seemed better.

Saturday Dec. 6: The ground is covered with snow tonight for the first. Begun about 5:00 o'clock and still snowing. Rec'd word today that Aunt Mary [may have been a sister of Irene's Mother but it was not Leonard's sister. Like the name Kate, there are a lot of Marys in the family.] in Katskill passed away yesterday. Ray went down tonight after a fellow he knows is coming up with him.

Sunday Dec 7: A nice day today. We did not go to church. Ray had a boy he knows come up. He went back tonight. Richters did not go home today is snowy and slippery. They brought the phonograph down played a lot on it. Aunt Mary's funeral was today.

Monday Dec 8: School started again today, Marjorie Cousins is teacher. I like her very much. She learned us a lot too. Richters board to our house yet they aren't going away until Saturday or Sunday unless it rains then.

Tuesday Dec 9: A nice day today. I was to school. Marjorie read a psalm out of the Bible and had Lord's Prayer. I play the phonograph a lot, we have 92 records. We can keep it all winter anyhow.

Wednesday Dec 10: A rainsome day today. I was to school. Marjorie read out of Bible as usual. Grocerman was here today. Mrs. Richter was down tonight & we play Authors. I beat 2 games and Mother one.

Thursday Dec 11: Quite a nice day today. I was to school. Teacher read a psalm today. Mrs. Richter was down with Mother most all day today helped her bake and do some work. Mother baked some crullers and fruit cake today and a angel food. Ray caught a fox this a.m.

Friday Dec 12: A gloomy day, rain this a.m. Mother was down to the village with Richters this p.m., didn't get back till 20 of 5. Got some things for to give away for Christmas. I was to school today. Marjorie read a psalm today.

Saturday Dec 13: A rainy day today. I have been playing the phonograph some today. Ray went down with Mr. Richter with his fox skin to get his bounty tonight. They say it was a wood gray.

Sunday Dec 14: A snowy day today. Richters did not go back it snowed so they couldn't. Ray got ice and Mrs. Richter & I pick out some nuts and we had walnut ice cream.

Monday Dec 15: A funny day today. I was to school. Teacher read today. Mr. & Mrs. Richter went back today. Mother washed. Certainly seems lonely without Richters here tonight.

Tuesday Dec. 16: A nice day today. I was to school. Teacher read in Bible today. We drawed names to get things for each other for Christmas at school today. I got Kenneth Reynolds. Have to give him something. I am going to speak a couple pieces. Marjorie stayed to my house all night tonight.

Wednesday Dec.17: A cold day today. Marjorie went back with me to school. The boys got a Christmas tree for the school today. We are going to take Richter's phonograph to school house the night we have speaking & aren't going to let the kids no till then.

Thursday Dec 18: A awful cold day today, 9 below zero this a.m. I was to school. We all had benches to set on around the fire to keep warm so cold in school. I took my Santa Clause and some trimmings for the Xmas tree to school this a.m.

Friday Dec.19: A snowy day today. I was to school today and noon time Dick Reynolds (Marjorie's fellow) took some of us kids to Saugerties and when we got back is was 1:05 and the kids that had stayed at school house went thinking we weren't coming back. Got an Xmas present from Orpha today but musn't break in till Xmas. [Imagine what would happen today if the teacher's boy friend came to school and took a group of her students for a day-long jaunt?]

Saturday Dec 20: A nice day today. Ray, Mother and I was to Saugerties. My teacher was ill so I couldn't take my music lesson. I took a cake all fixed up and some cake and eggs for Xmas.

Sunday Dec. 21: A snowy day today. We did not go to church because Ray worked down in the dairy farm down to Caldwells. We done up a lot of packages today to send away.

Monday Dec 22: A nice day today growing warmer. I was to school. Ray, Mother and I rec'd packages tonight. Ray's and Mother's where registered. Also a package from Aunt Esther for us all. A dollar in for me. Also a package from Lute and Cora.

Tuesday Dec. 23: A nice day today, much warmer. I was to school. Ray took our phonograph down to the entertainment tonight. We had a big crowed—31 and Santa Claus was Dick Reynolds and he was a dandy. I got 2 tablets and 2 pencils. Rec'd a package from Merkles today can't open it till Xmas.

Wednesday Dec 24: A nice day today, getting colder tonight. I was to school today. There will be no more school till Jan. 5. Teacher give us each a card today for Xmas. Mother rec'd a parcel from Mary my teacher today, 2 handkerchiefs. I rec'd 1 also but haven't opened it yet. Art & Evadora coming tonight.

Thursday Dec. 25: Been a lovely day. 12 presents and 2 stockings full of things from Santa. Arthur & Evadora & Ernie where here. Ray went back with A. & E. to Hurly to E's folks.

Friday Dec. 26: A nice day today. Viola was up to my house this p.m. and Aunt Katherine and Anna was down. Viola and I rode downhill.

Saturday Dec. 27: A nice day today. Ray went to Saugerties tonight but I did not go as I couldn't take a lesson as my teacher wasn't home. Mother and I was playing a game I got for Xmas.

Sunday Dec. 28: A nice day today. We was to church. I spoke 2 pieces and they give all the children who spoke an orange and some candy. We went in to Aunt Kate's for dinner. Irving has a nice Xmas tree.

Monday Dec 29: A nice day but awful cold. Mother washed. Ray went to his work. Got a silk handkerchief from Julia Meyers for my Xmas today.

Tuesday Dec. 30: Snowed this forenoon but cleared off this afternoon. We went up to Aunt Katharine's this p.m. She helped Ma make a dress for me that Mrs. Richter gave me goods for.

Wednesday Dec. 31: A nice day today. We haven't no school, won't have until Jan.5. Stolls called over and I and the girls rode downhill. This is last of my dear old book, haven't any for another year So Goodbye.

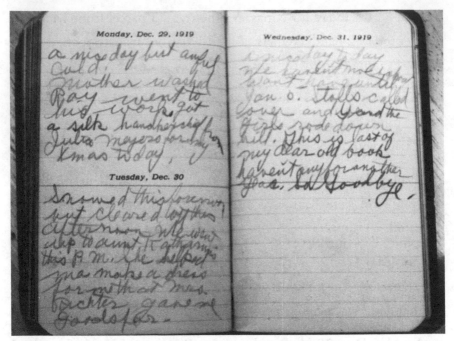

Last three entries of Catharine's Diary

AFTERWORD

On June 23, 1922, at the Pine Grove School, Ulster County awarded 13-year old Catharine Mae Snyder a Common School Diploma; it was signed by Helen R Keenan, teacher. At the comparable point in their lives all the rest of the Snyder siblings were done with their formal education—only Ray would, later in his life, get his GED—but not Catharine. For whatever reason and at least against the wishes of her sister Elizabeth, Catharine matriculated in Saugerties High School that fall. This was not easy for a 13-year old girl to get up every morning and ride the horse and buggy/sleigh five or so miles into school each day. Accidents happened.

That winter, with Ray driving, the trace on the harness broke, scaring the horse so that he jumped the fountain in the square in Saugerties and dumped the sleigh. Catharine and her books ended up in a snow bank. While Ray went after the horse, Catharine went into a saloon nearby where the early morning patrons helped her locate her school books.

By this time Ray was married, a baby was on the way and, presumably, he could no longer help as much on the farm. He would soon follow his siblings and leave Pine Grove, in his case for Kingston. At some point between 1923 and 1926, the widow Snyder sold her farm and, with her daughter Elizabeth, moved into Kingston as well. (I am not sure exactly when this move took place but I do have Irene's 1926 diary. Judging from the entries, she was living in Kingston and had been there for some time.) At any rate, in 1924 Catharine left Pine Grove and moved in with a family in Saugerties where she worked as a maid and babysat their children. This would be the first of two families she lived with during the remaining three years of high school. Excepting for visits prior to her mother's move she never lived again at Pine Grove.

Unfortunately, the names of the families for whom she worked are lost in time. I do remember they were fairly well off and at least once or twice she took us past the large, well cared for homes where she had worked at what was, essentially, an au pair job. I also know that one of her duties at one home was to clean fireplaces because, even in her eighties, when we added some woodstoves to our home she warned us they could be messy. I know too that the people she worked for were very understanding and they did whatever they could to make her school life pleasant. They may well have been related to her family.

In 1926, at the age of seventeen, she graduated at the top of her class at Saugerties High School and was accepted at Albany State Teachers College as a 4-year candidate in foreign language education. Her plans, as noted in the SHS Class of 1926 prophecy, were to be a high school language teacher. Between semesters at Albany she returned to her mother's home in Kingston where she was, with Elizabeth's help and encouragement, employed as a waitress in a local restaurant. Early on her temper almost cost her this job when, upon being told to do something a certain way by the chef, she asked "Who has died and left you boss?" She rapidly learned where a seasonally employed waitress fell in the hierarchy of the restaurant business.

Fulfilling her high school prophecy, she graduated in 1930 and took a job that September teaching French at Roessleville High School in Albany. Three years later she began dating the school's athletic director/coach. On June 27, 1934, in the rectory of the Christ Lutheran Church in Woodstock, she married Herchel Mortensen; the son of a Danish immigrant father and second generation German mother who had come east from Minnesota. Also, sometime between graduation from high school and college her name metamorphosed from Catharine to Kate to Kay. This last was how she would be known by her husband, his family and all her friends and acquaintances for the rest of her life. Even her two sons, whenever they introduced her, would call her Kay. It was only her Snyder siblings and their children who continued to call her Catharine.

Seven years later Kay, now the mother of two boys, would return to the Hudson Valley where she would remain for the next third of her life. First she lived in Tivoli, a village on the east side of the river almost directly across from Saugerties. Two years later, the family moved a little further north to Germantown. The town which grew up near East Camp was named after those people who settled the area, her ancestors, the Palatines. (There is strong evidence that an older brother of Martin, named Juris or Johannes Snyder may have settled on the east side of the Hudson with the first of the Palatines in 1710.) Germantown would be where she would eventually go back to teaching—this time junior high school mathematics. By 1962 she had accumulated enough graduate hours to be awarded a Masters Degree in Education from SUNY Albany. She taught in Germantown Central School until her retirement in 1972. At that time she and her husband moved from the

Hudson River for the last time, resettling in Oxford, NY, where she lived until she died in 2008. Catharine is buried beside Herchel in the Riverside Cemetery in Oxford.

While in Germantown, Herchel and Kay built a small 6-room house on County Route 8 about two miles east of the village. Behind the house was a large wooded ridge that stood between our home and the Roeliff Jensen Kill. About a third of the way up this ridge was a hay field the locals called the "Green Spot". In the middle of this field was an outcropping of the limestone bedrock that we would hike to and have picnics on because it was a great place to get a view of "The Old Man of The Mountain". From this part of the Hudson Valley the Catskill Mountains align in such a way that, from our vantage point and with very little imagination, one can see the profile of a man lying with his feet to the south, knees bent, arms on his chest and head, with his nose sticking straight up, to the north. It was always understood that the better you could see him, the better the weather was going to be and if he wasn't visible, you'd better head home because it was going to rain. It wasn't until years later when I was looking over some topographic maps that I realized that those knees were actually Overlook Mountain and, when my mother looked at The Old Man, something she would do every clear day on her way to work, she was actually looking right past her old home in Pine Grove. I don't think she ever knew.

About Leonard

There are three things my generation of Snyder's have speculated about but never have gotten definitive answers for: the cause of Ernie's mental retardation, Elizabeth's love life and Leonard's insanity. While I am not sure about the first two, from Catharine's diary and the way her life progressed I may have an answer for the third. The evidence would strongly suggest that Leonard suffered from the same kind of dementia that finally robbed Catharine of her mind and life by her 99th year.

The story about Leonard varies but supposedly his "spells" were either brought on or stopped when he was kicked in the head by a mule. While I doubt the mule story, after reading Catharine's diary and from the preceding mule statements it would seem these spells were intermittent and, as time went on, increased in frequency until, finally they just did not go away. (It should also be noted that the decision to send him to the asylum was made by his immediate family, apparently, because they could no longer care for him. This caused a rift between Irene and Leonard's brothers, primarily Franklin, which isolated her and her children from the rest of the family.)

This is the kind of thing that happened to Catharine starting at about the age of 95, often triggered by a unitary tract infection—I can't help but note that prior to Leonard's first bout both he and his wife were sick with something. Like Leonard, she began with bouts of anxiety, followed by hallucinations and finally loss of long-term memory. By the age of 97, Catherine was completely lost from us.

Of course, at 60, Leonard was younger than Catharine when it started but he did not have the benefit of diet, medical attention and mental exercise that she had. If mental exercise can ward off brain deterioration then she certainly held it at bay. She was a great puzzle solver, and for years her favorite was the Word Jumble. If you aren't familiar with this puzzle, it has 4 clue-words of 5 to 8 letters each that are jumbled up. The player has to unscramble the letters and write the words in a series of boxes, one letter per box. Some of these boxes have circles in them. The puzzle also includes a cartoon with a quote pertaining to the cartoon that is missing a word or two or three. The number of letters missing in the quote corresponds to the number of circles in the clue-word boxes. To solve the whole puzzle one first unscrambles the clue-words, then use the letters in the circles, to solve the rest of the quote. It is not easy to do but Catharine thrived on it. In fact, rather than write out the clue-words, she just filled in the circles. From the time she was in her sixty's until she reached her mid90's, she never started her day without doing the Jumble and, if for some reason, the paper didn't print one or hid it in a different place in the paper she was on the phone to them. After the Jumble, she was on to the daily crossword and any other puzzle she could lay her hands on—she loved Magic Squares where numbers had to add down, across and diagonally to the same sum. At about 94, however, the Jumbles went unsolved and her crossword puzzles unfinished. Gradually, she could only do the "circle the word" puzzles and, by 95 they were too hard. It was at this point she was no longer able to care for herself. As I read through the diary I see the same progression in Leonard as I saw with her and it leads me to believe that this tendency may be in us all. As the saying goes, "Growing old isn't for cowards."

Religion

As a group, the Palatines were, by and large, Protestants, primarily Lutherans or Dutch Reformed. While there were some Catholics among the immigrants, most kept that knowledge to themselves until they landed in North America, probably due to the fear of retaliation by the other members of the group. There certainly would have been rationalization for this inasmuch as there had been a great deal of conflict between the two groups in Germany and elsewhere. This left a legacy of discrimination and mistrust between Protestants and Catholics that continued into Catharine's childhood. Simply no one would consider marrying a Catholic or even closely dealing with one.

While Catharine was brought up in the Lutheran Church, she spent most of her life moving from one sect to another. She married a Congregationalist and they had joined the Presbyterian Church by the time her sons were baptized. When the family moved to Tivoli they lived in the Episcopal rectory so she went there to church. Upon moving to Germantown she came back to Martin's church, the Dutch Reformed, where she taught Sunday school as well as Vacation Bible School. After retirement and the move to Oxford, she and her husband became Methodist which continued until his death. Finally she joined a fundamentalist, bible based sect and helped establish the Faith Bible Church in Oxford. All this time, regardless of to whichever group she belonged, she had a great deal of faith. For one thing, if you ever disputed her on any biblical quote or passage, you did it at your own peril and the chance of being proved wrong.

I once asked her what made her do what she did with her life: go on to high school and college which meant moving away from home.

Her answer was "faith". Apparently at some point in her childhood her pastor told her she had the ability to go on to become someone of importance if she believed she could. This guided her throughout her life.

Irene's Wedding Photo

Leonard and Irene's wedding photo

Elizabeth and Catharine c1915

Dot Merkel (l) and Catharine c1921

Pine Grove School c1908: Ray is dead center, third from the left in the second row (dark shirt), and the girl in back row, left end (dark jumper) is Elizabeth.

Catharine's HS Graduation photo

Photo along Stoll Rd. c1935

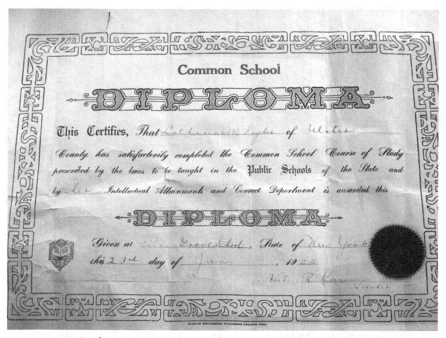

Catharine's Diploma from Pine Grove School

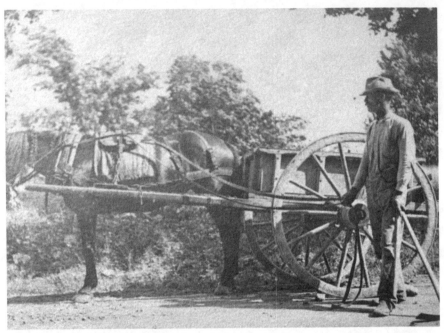

Leonard with 2-wheeled cart

Load of cut bluestone—Uncle Raym is to the left

Pine Grove School in 2009—sign says "Pine Grove School 1839"

Lutheran Church in Woodstock

Catharine's Family Tree

Martin Snyder –Anna Demuth Backer

/ \

Jeremiah Snyder—Catharine Holly   Zachariah Snyder—Margaret Fiero

/   /

Elias Snyder—Margaret Hommel   Margaret Snyder—Fredrick Cunyes

/   /

Jeremiah Elias Snyder—Catherine VanVlierden   William Henry Cunyes—Margaret Shultis

/   /

Elias Snyder—Eliza Christina Lasher   Stanford Cunyes—Sarah Elizabeth Herrick

\   /

Leonard Snyder   Irene Cunyes

\   /

Catharine May Snyder

Reference:

Books

Evers, Alf, The Catskills From Wilderness to Woodstock, revised and updated, c1982, The Overlook Press, Woodstock NY

Evers, Alf, Kingston, City on the Hudson, c2005 , The Overlook Press, Woodstock NY

Evers, Alf, Woodstock, History of an American Town, c1987, The Overlook Press, Woodstock NY

Knittle Phd, Walter Allen, Early Eighteenth Century Palestine Emigration, c1965, Genealogical Publishing Co., Baltimore

Shorto, Russell, Island at the Center of the World, The Epic of Dutch Manhattan and the Forgotten Colony That Shaped America, c2005, Vintage Books, New York

Internet

Palatines of America—German Genealogy Society, www.palam. org

Palatine Research by Lorine McGinnis Schulze, c1996 Olive Tree Enterprises, www.rootsweb.com

Names for the Dutch Language, Wikipedia, The Free Encyclopedia,

German Palatines, Wikipedia, The Free Encyclopedia

Narratives and Adventures of Revolutionary Prisoners, From The Catskill Mountains and the Region Around by Rev. Charles Rockwell, c1867, Catskill Archive, www.catskillarchive.com/rockwell

Printed in the United States
by Baker & Taylor Publisher Services